KISSING
EZRA HOLTZ
(AND OTHER THINGS I DID FOR SCIENCE)

Also by Brianna R. Shrum
Never Never
How to Make Out
The Art of French Kissing

KISSING
EZRA HOLTZ
(AND OTHER THINGS I DID FOR SCIENCE)

Brianna R. Shrum

Sky Pony Press
New York

Sky Pony Press books may be purchased in bulk at special discounts for
sales promotion, corporate gifts, fund-raising, or educational purposes.
Special editions can also be created to specifications. For details,
contact the Special Sales Department, Sky Pony Press, 307 West 36th
Street, 11th Floor, New York, NY 10018 or info@skyhorsepublishing.com.

Sky Pony® is a registered trademark of Skyhorse Publishing, Inc.®,
a Delaware corporation.

Visit our website at www.skyponypress.com.

10 9 8 7 6 5 4 3 2 1

This product conforms to CPSIA 2008

Library of Congress Cataloging-in-Publication Data is available on file.

Cover design by Kate Gartner
Cover photo credit iStock

Hardcover ISBN: 978-1-5107-4940-5
Ebook ISBN: 978-1-5107-4373-1

Printed in the United States of America.

For every one of you who has ever believed you are playing a supporting role in your own life. You are the main character.

CHAPTER ONE

Hypothesis (n.): A prediction or claim based on observed evidence, which warrants future testing

Example: If high school is a microcosm of the world, then I am doomed to fail at every venture I give a single crap about until the day I die.

Supporting Evidence: EVERYTHING.

The first thing Ezra Holtz says to me this morning is, "How did you even get into this class?"

Of course he does. Everyone else in this classroom is pairing up, no complaints. The perfect little AP students. But not Ezra.

Not when he's been condemned to me.

I roll my eyes and look down at my nails, chipping gray polish on one hand, peeling black on the other. I'm instantly pissed, but not like it's a surprise, coming from him. Ezra and I have gone to the same synagogue since we were kids, and he's never exactly been relaxed and humble. Still, 7:45 a.m. is too early for this.

1

Honestly, it's too early for *Ezra*.

I keep my eyes on my fingers when I say, "Same way you did, Holtz."

I see his jaw tighten out of the corner of my eye, see his long fingers tap against his forearms. "Somehow I doubt that."

"Alright," I say. "I blackmailed my way in. I begged. I paid a counselor fifty bucks to please, *please* allow me the honor of attending AP psychology this semester, god, I'll do *anything*."

He blows out a breath through his nose, which he only does when he's really, really frustrated. I don't even try not to smile.

"Honestly, man, sit down," I say, kicking the chair next to me.

Ezra glances up toward the front of the classroom, like maybe if he catches Mr. Yeun's eye, he will relieve Ezra from this nightmare. Then, when he isn't even granted a half-second of eye contact, he sits. Really, he sinks. Into a perfect straight-backed ninety degree with his lap. He sighs and finally deigns to look me in the eye. "Look, Amalia, this grade is important to me. Crucially, critically—"

"Redundantly importantly. I get it."

He blinks.

"I, uh—"

I wait.

He says, "I don't dislike you or something. It's just that I need this."

He needs this. Like I don't?

"Maybe . . ." He glances around, because what he is about to say is definitely going to be irritating enough that he doesn't want anyone else to hear. "Maybe it would be best if you let me take point on the project."

I smile as sweetly as I can manage. It's a smile I've honed over the years, just for him. I say, "Not a chance."

He glances up at the ceiling tiles and smooths his hand down his dark green button-down. A button-down. In the twelfth grade.

This is a public school.

It would have the potential to be charming if the head and body attached to it weren't constantly adjusting their glasses so that they could properly look down at everyone in visual range.

Ezra says, "Fine. But if you aren't pulling your weight, I'm not letting my chances at valedictorian falter because of it."

"I don't even know what that means. Is that a threat?"

His lips thin. And he says, "Yes."

My mouth turns up. "Get better at that."

"Excuse me?"

"If someone has to ask if it's a threat, well, it's not very threatening, is it?"

"Amalia."

"Holtz."

"I'm just saying that if you're going to work with me, you work."

I do nothing to disguise the irritation that flashes across my face.

I don't think I've ever had to speak with him on my own for this long. Usually after five minutes of being forced together in temple, one of us has made some excuse to go to the bathroom or find a roaming-the-halls sibling or ask a pressing question of the rabbi. We've both spent an inordinate amount of time asking ridiculous questions of the poor guy to avoid each other without either of our parents suspecting we're being assholes about it. My mom must think I am the most religiously curious kid in the world. That I actually wanted to know if it would be possible for a vampire to keep kosher. I do wind up thinking about these things an awful lot, but it's for the excuses file, more than anything. So what I'm saying is, generally, one of us has found the means to escape conversation by this point. I've never quite tested it for this long. My reserves are running thin.

I say, "My turn, then."

"For what?"

"To tell you that if you're going to work with me, you can work *with* me. Maybe I care about this class, too. Yeah, I know, scrape your jaw off the floor."

Ezra swallows and glances down at the desk, at the other pairs of kids who are talking, actively, planning everything out. He can't stand being behind.

We're paired on a project that will span an entire quarter—a psychology study we formulate and test and then finally we write an essay and give a presentation about the conclusions we found. It's a huge part of the overall class grade, so I get why he's sweating.

But I'm sweating, too.

I push my blonde-brown tangle of curly hair behind my shoulders and say, "I need this grade just as much as you do."

He raises a dark brown eyebrow. "Do you?"

"Yes. I'm not gonna entrust you with my grade any more than you'll trust me with yours."

He snorts and, I swear, I am *this close* to climbing over my desk and squeezing his arrogant throat.

"I swear to god, Holtz," is what I say instead, but if he so much as ticks a lip, I'm going to do it.

He says, "Okay. No, of course. I just thought maybe you'd rather—anyway. I'm sorry. Let's do this together." He has to say, "Obviously," through his teeth.

I dig my notebook out of the black hole that is my backpack and something twitches in that sharp jaw of his when he glances at it.

But I open it, manage to find an unmarred page, and we get started.

After the last bell, I duck into the closest bathroom and shrug out of my plaid overshirt and ripped skinnies and into shorts and a T-shirt. Items of clothing that don't smell like smoke from lunch.

Then, I head to the counselor's office. Ezra and I basically have nothing to go off of. All his ideas are the most boring, paint-by-numbers shit. Surveying kids about their testing habits. Having a group of adults take a self-analysis, then compare those with their political preferences in order to predict political affiliation by personality type. Stuff that's literally making me drowsy just thinking about it.

He shut down basically all my ideas, on account of them not being quantifiable enough or being too invasive.

Testing people's personal bubbles and breaking it down by demographic, measuring emotion based on viewing different kinds of art, listening to music.

Every other human I saw leaving the class had a list by the end.

We? Have an 8x11's worth of illegible ink. Everything's been crossed out.

I let out an aggrieved sigh and push open Mr. Ilyas's door.

"Amalia!"

I smile and set down my backpack.

"You're early."

"I'm on time," I say, glancing behind me at the clock which reads 2:59.

"Like I said," he says with a little smile, "early."

I think I have developed . . . something of a reputation. Which was not necessarily intentional, but it's not like it was entirely unintentional either.

It's not as though you can cut class that many times, hang out at smoker's corner (with weed or otherwise) that many lunch periods, and flee from that many parties the second before the cops show up and not know what people are going to think of you.

"So," he says.

"So."

"I'm looking over your grades and your planned classes, and honestly, Amalia, if we're going to bump this up, it's . . . well, you're going to have to drastically change some things."

I swallow hard. "I—yeah. Yeah I know. But I can do this, I swear I can."

6

"It's my job to help you succeed. I don't want to give you all these transfers to advanced classes and find that I've thrown you into the deep end of the pool and you can't swim."

"I can *swim*, Mr. Ilyas. I can swim. I mean . . . I can do the work."

He levels a look at me.

Neither of us says what we both know: that my failure as a student is entirely on me.

I screwed around for three years, threw my entire life into art, all of my dreams into art school, and when it came down to it, I wasn't good enough. Every school I applied to shot me down. I didn't even have freaking backups, I was so certain.

"What are your academic plans following high school?" he says.

My mouth is dry and my palms start to sweat. Nothing is more terrifying than that question. I am afraid that I screwed up my entire high school career. Wanting to be an *artist*. Knowing I could. Showing up late to math and lit and ditching out during physics and just skating through these difficult classes like they didn't matter, because who cared?

I *tried* in my art classes. I worked my ass off in every last one of them.

Here's the thing.

I am smart. I know I'm smart. Smart enough I was put into all this gifted shit as a little kid, and it stayed that way through middle school, and it's not like these classes in high school have been hard.

But how these other AP kids and *future valedictorians* find it in their souls to put in two hours of homework a night when it's not like it matters—it's not like they're gonna fail the test even if they don't study—is beyond me.

I knock every test out of the park.

Even in the classes I barely show up to.

I just—why was I supposed to care? About the other boring crap—homework and class participation and puzzling out the meaning of all the metaphors in "The Lottery"? I was going to art school.

I blink down at Mr. Ilyas's laminate desk.

I am not going to art school.

Here's the irony of it: if I'd participated in class—shown up, even—if I'd just literally ever done my homework . . . If I'd, as a result, had good enough grades to go along with those less-than-prodigy-level art pieces I applied with, they might have been enough to bump me up. Grant me provisional admittance or something.

Ilyas and my parents and my siblings—well, just Kaylee, really—have even reminded me of this. I know. But I can't turn back time.

And the situation is this: I can't go to art school. I'm in the running for *Most Artistic* this year and I can't go.

So I have to do something else.

"Mr. Ilyas," I say, "please, please just believe in me. Swap out English and chemistry for AP. Look at my test grades again; I can hack it. If I can't, you can roll me back into something else at midterms. But I can't do what I—" I choke. "What I wanted to do, and so I have to have the opportunity to be something else."

Mr. Ilyas looks down at my test scores, all laid out in front of him.

He rubs his forehead, cleans his glasses.

He says, "I'm going to do this for you. But you will show me that you can handle it. Is that understood?"

"Yes," I say on a desperate breath. "Thank you."

I'm grateful for the opportunity to work my ass off my entire senior year, so I can fix my grades and get into a good program that is not art, somewhere that is not here.

I almost laugh when I leave.

There's this ball of anxiety in my chest, comingled with hope and appreciation and . . . I don't even know for what.

CHAPTER TWO

Observation: An organism is designed for its particular habitat. To survive and contribute to its ecosystem. If you move a fish from water to land, that fish will die. Take a sled dog out of the tundra and drop him into Ecuador, he may survive, but he's not going to look pretty when he gets there. In other words: Change is the enemy.

Ezra texts me the second I get home. Probably just got out of math league or academic decathlon or debate or . . . who knows what Smart Thing That Overachievers Do.

Ezra: What about something in video games?

I cock my head.

Amalia: You have my attention.

Ezra: We could have people chart the
hours they play.

Three little dots that show he's typing a second message.

I write back before he can finish.

> **Amalia:** Charting hours. How on earth have you managed to make VIDEO GAMES boring

He stops typing.
Starts again.
Stops.

> **Amalia:** Let's recreate the Stanford Prison Experiment.
> **Ezra:** Haha.
> **Ezra:** You are hilarious.

I can hear the deadpan through the screen.

> **Ezra:** I'm not trying to be boring. I'm trying to nail a surefire thing.

I sigh. It is aggrieved. It is long, long suffering.

> **Amalia:** Listen, I'm exhausted. Are you gonna be at shul tomorrow night?
> **Ezra:** I can be.
> **Amalia:** Let's just meet up after.

No response.
After five minutes, I send:

> **Amalia:** A single day without preparation isn't gonna kill you.

Five more minutes later:

Ezra: Fine.

I smirk. Getting under his skin has always been at least a little satisfying.

My big brother hops up behind me on the couch and says, "Boyfriend?" He waggles his wildly unkempt eyebrows.

"Ugh. No."

"Girlfriend?"

"Also no."

"Anyfriend?" He hops over the back of it and plants his butt on the cushion beside me. I have to move my feet so he doesn't crush them.

"Ezra Holtz."

"Ezra *Holtz*? Why the hell."

"He's not that bad."

He laughs out a disbelieving, "Okay," just as my little sister says, "I like Ezra."

"Of course you do, nerd," says Ben.

She wrinkles her nose. "One of us around here has to be."

"Well," says Ben, "Amalia's at least half-nerd."

I purse my lips and catch Kaylee's eye. She shoots me back a grin. There is a particular kind of constant conspiracy that only sisters really get. She's three years younger than I am and a total Hermione Granger—different than me in basically every way. Smooth hair where mine is wild (and I like it that way). Light brown eyeliner if any, where mine is smoky and black. She lives and dies by the CW and history documentaries, and if I'm watching TV at all, it's music biopics and the kind of violent, weird nature stuff that they only air at 2 a.m. We're different. But she gets it.

I glance back down at my phone when Ben and Kaylee start in on each other about who's supposed to do the dishes next and how Ben feels like ever since he graduated high school but stayed at home, he's been saddled with extra chores and why should he be punished for being fiscally responsible.

Ezra's *fine* blinks up at me.

I can hear him sighing, see that little glasses adjustment that says he's disappointed, but not enough to verbalize it.

Lord.

This is going to be a long semester.

⚗

My adjusted schedule stares back at me from my inbox: AP. AP. AP. Gym. Because I have limits. Panic crawls up my throat in an unfamiliar way and I hate it. Just looking at all of this is like one of those dreams where you show up to school and realize you've been ditching for two months and now OH NO, it's the final!

This is. A lot.

I guess I'm doing it though.

On purpose.

I sigh and move to open the syllabi for a bunch of brand new classes I'm going to have to actually work to survive, and my phone buzzes.

Sasha: I'm bored
Amalia: Have a nap.
Sasha: Fix it.

I smirk.

> **Amalia:** I'm not a WIZARD, Sash.
> **Sasha:** Help us, Amalia, you're our only
> hope.

I'm still smiling, already grabbing my jacket and hunting for my keys when I type back:

> **Amalia:** Honestly where would ANY of your
> lives be without me. I'm coming to
> save you.
> **Sasha:** BLESS YOU.
> **Sasha:** We're at Keegan's.

I have no clue what "we" means, but it doesn't really matter. Sasha means Brent, and Keegan for sure, and anyone involved in that group means a good time.

I head for my bedroom door and catch the syllabi in my periphery.

I should be looking over them, just to see what I've missed in the last week and a half. Overachieving, showing Ilyas how invested I am or whatever.

Eh. I haven't even *started* these classes yet. It'll be fine.

I head out the door.

🜾

"Cards?" Sasha wrinkles her nose and side-eyes the deck in my hand.

"No complaining," I say. "You invited me here."

"To make it a *party*," Brent mumbles.

"It's a Thursday night, you cretins."

There are eleven of us here, just enough to call it a party if you wanted. Not enough to really tip into rager territory. The ideal mid-week hangout.

Sasha's best friend, Asia, raises both hands in the air and says, "Everyone hush your mouths." She tips her chin at me. "Go."

"Deck of cards," I say. "Brent, go grab some spoons out of the silverware drawer and bring down some liquor."

Brent—Letter Jacket Brent if I'm feeling mean; he never takes the thing off. I sometimes wonder if he wears it while he and Sasha are hooking up—says, "Nope. If my dad wouldn't kill me for getting into the tequila, we wouldn't have required your services."

I draw my hand to my chest. "I'm wounded."

"Wouldn't have *required*," says Sasha. "But would have invited."

Some girl I don't know says, "Tequila. Gross."

"So Brent's afraid of Dad. Okay. You afraid to borrow some spoons, sport?"

He scowls at me but heads upstairs to the kitchen.

Brent's basement is familiar. It's huge and tricked out. Big screen TV, pool table, couple of guest bedrooms that I have *never* seen used for *sleeping*. All the finishes are shiny and new, too, kind of like basically everyone's clothes—preppy rich friends. Sports, student council, that crowd.

I recline on Brent's fancy Italian leather sofa (for a teen basement, seriously) and ignore the twinge of disappointment in my stomach that says, *No, you are not getting top shelf liquor this evening.*

Brent stomps down the stairs, still looking a little peeved, and hands me a fistful of spoons.

"So?" says Asia.

"The game is Spoons." I explain the rules, which basically consist of throwing a bunch of spoons in the middle of a circle, then passing cards around in various ways until someone gets four of a kind. First one to get it grabs a spoon. Last one left without one drinks.

"We can't drink," says Sasha, elbowing Brent, who groans and bites her neck. She shrieks.

"What a shame," I say.

Pasty Travis, whom I don't love, honestly, but there's always one in a group, says, "What does that mean?"

My mouth curls. "Well. We all have clothes, don't we?"

Brent slowly raises an eyebrow and Sasha says, "Strip Spoons? Strip Spoons."

"Strip Spoons. Grab your cards."

It takes a minute, but eventually, everyone acquiesces. Asia, who has a weave that falls down to her waist and legs for actual days, bumps my shoulder and says, "Strip Spoons. You slut."

I grin. It's a word I've heard . . . a number of times, directed at me. It doesn't hurt coming from her. Because 1) she's my friend, 2) she's a girl (who gets my pulse spiking every time she sits this close), and 3) she has a reputation, too.

Some guy a couple seats down from Asia says, under his breath, "So I've heard."

And that feels a hell of a lot different.

Asia cuts a glance at me and I give her one terse head shake. Not worth it.

She purses her lips and scoots just a little closer, and the game starts. It's a racket of cards and shrieks and body parts bumping into body parts and by the end of it, we're all in various stages of undress, I've wound up with my tongue down Asia's throat like twice, Brent and Sasha are making out, someone's turned on some music, and it may as well be a real party.

Who knows where Brent's parents are when the clock hits 1 a.m., but they're not here, and I'm getting sleepy but I'm alive. Wired on all of my friends and the adrenaline that comes from this many people in this small room, all just happily coexisting.

I love this.

Everyone is extremely welcome that I left my studying at home and showed up.

CHAPTER THREE

Fight or Flight Response (n.): The instinctive response aroused in the human brain when presented with acute terror or stress that causes either the instinct to flee or to fight for one's survival via the release of epinephrine and/or norepinephrine.

Synonyms:
> *Hyperarousal*
> *Acute Stress Response*
> *Existence in Mr. Thompson's Military Barracks of an AP Chemistry Classroom*

I stumble into AP chemistry like I'm hung over. I'm not, not from alcohol anyway. But from lack of sleep? Well. It turns out that's a thing.

The teacher, who is former military and has the haircut and attitude to match, raises his eyebrow. "Amalia Yaabez."

I shrug off my backpack into a chair in the farthest corner of the room.

"Why don't you sit up front?" he says.

I purse my lips. "A/C is up there. I don't want to get cold."

He smiles sweetly. "The cold will keep you awake."

My nostrils flare and I wrap my fingers around the strap of my bag. I say through clenched teeth, "In chemistry? Why would I need something to keep me up?"

Mr. Thompson's mouth curls up and he says, "Yaabez?"

"Mmhmm."

"Have a seat."

He kicks the seat in the front and center of the classroom and it physically hurts not to roll my eyes. I would like to note, for the record, that despite my no-sleep-party-night hangover, I am the first kid here.

That should count for something.

Guess it doesn't.

The only nice thing about this morning is that one of the girls I smoke with sometimes shows up (she, too, was assigned to sit up front) and parks beside me.

She waggles her eyebrows. "Ready for some fun?"

"Oh," I say, deadpan, "I was born ready."

She laughs and then turns forward when Thompson starts lecturing. I'm surprised to see Marisol here, I guess. Not that kids who smoke weed can't be smart—I mean, I'm in here. But—well, there's really no explanation that doesn't make me seem like a weirdly hypocritical asshole so I don't think too much about it.

People contain multitudes.

I don't think about Marisol and worlds colliding.

I think—I *try* to think—about chemistry. About the things that make up the entire universe. I lean back in my chair so no one thinks I'm panicking. Throw my arm over the plastic so I look like I belong here, like I'm comfortable.

Like always.

But I am not comfortable.

I *am* panicking.

AP chemistry, what was I thinking?

I've only missed like a week of the class and I already feel like I have no idea what the hell he's saying. Maybe this was a mistake. Maybe it was all a mistake.

I'm blinking at the white board, focusing so hard on not knowing shit that I miss it when he calls on me the first time. I must miss *several*, because when he finally gets my attention, it seems like he's been trying for a while. The classroom is that specific kind of quiet that seems like they're waiting for something.

Hushed.

"I'm sorry. What?"

Thompson, fucking sadist, says, "You heard me."

I scoff. Like it doesn't matter. I say, "Sorry, I didn't."

"Guess."

"Two."

A wave of snickers. I lean back farther. Put my foot up on the desk. All of my resolve to fix everything this semester is crumbling under scrutiny. Under this sudden humiliating pressure.

He says, "Guess again."

I say, "I don't know what the *fuck* you said."

Thompson smiles. "I said *detention*. Hope you don't have plans after school for the next week."

I narrow my eyes.

And pull out my pencil. "So. Two? Was that the answer?"

He grinds his teeth. It's like he's forgotten we're not the only ones in here. That's fine. I haven't.

"The answer. Was carbon. Unless the question was how many extra days of detention you're landing yourself every time you open your mouth."

I stand.

I glance over his shoulder at the white board and I don't get any of it, I don't care about any of it, who the hell cares.

I stick my headphone in one of my ears.

I leave.

My parents get a call from Mr. Thompson after school when I don't show for detention, and I hear my mom sigh from across the house. It's not like they're surprised. They can't be.

But I'm . . . god, I'm embarrassed by it. I'm actually *embarrassed* by my own behavior. And now I get to tell Ezra that I earned myself two weeks of detention because I couldn't be *quiet*. Lord. Turning over a new leaf is exhausting and impossible and I don't know how people do it.

Maybe they don't.

Maybe no one actually does.

I head to my room. I want to have this inevitable confrontation on my own turf.

"Amalia." Mom's voice rings up the stairs.

I run my hand over my nose. "Mmhmm?"

My mom walks up the stairs, quiet enough I can't hear her steps. She always walks on her tiptoes up the stairs; I don't know why. I run my hand through my hair.

"That was Mr. Thompson."

She appears in my doorway, crossed arms and graying hair and an eyebrow cocked.

I fling myself back on my bed and groan. "Mom, listen."

"Oh, I'm listening."

"He's—I'm sorry, I don't know how else to say this; Mr. Thompson is a dick."

I feel my mom's weight when she sits on the bed beside me. "*I don't know what the fuck you said*? Amalia, come on."

"You can't say that word in front of me. I'm your child." I sit up and look at her. She's trying not to smile.

"I can say whatever I want. I'm a grown-up."

The corner of my mouth tips. "A grown-up."

Now we're both laughing, but she reins it in pretty fast. "You can't say that kind of stuff in class."

"I know."

"I thought you were getting it together."

"I—" It catches in my throat. "I am."

She looks directly at me, gold-auburn eyebrow quirking up again. "Is this what getting it together looks like to you?"

I shrug. "I'm sorry. He was pushing me so hard, everyone knows he's horrible. I overreacted in class; it was disrespectful." I'm saying what she wants to hear and she knows it.

"I know. Listen, I spent five minutes on the phone with the man, and I get it. But you can't."

I sigh. Run my nails over my navy bedspread. "I know. I'm really sorry."

She runs her hand over my head in a generous display of mercy. "You've got to get this under control."

She means my hair, I think. I *think*. "I can't."

She smiles when I do. "I know."

"Don't tell Dad?"

She rolls her eyes and gets up. "We'll see."

"Hey," I say before she leaves my room, happy not to be saddled with a punishment. I guess she thinks two weeks' detention with that man is enough. I'm not gonna argue.

"Hmm?"

"Give me a ride to shul tonight?"

"I think we can make that happen."

She gives me this half-exasperated, half-affectionate look and leaves. I remind her of her, I think, and that gets me out of just . . . so much shit I should not get out of.

Like I said, I'm not gonna argue.

I'm . . . well. I'm gonna get dressed and go to temple.

CHAPTER FOUR

Dependent Variables: My ability to fix my shitstorm of an academic career—My senior GPA
My senior GPA—My grade in this AP Psychology class
My grade in this AP Psychology class—
My grade on this project
My grade on this project—My ability to refrain from murdering Ezra Holtz

About forty-five minutes into shul, the venti Frappuccino I had my parents run me through the coffee shop to get finally kicks in and I feel good about faking being awake. At least until I can kick Ezra out of my house and then immediately pass out on my bedroom floor.

After service, in which our rabbi looks just the slightest touch relieved that neither of us has any questions related to dietary laws and mythological creatures and just throws us both a half-confused "Good Shabbos," when we walk out together, *intentionally*, Ezra offers to drive me home.

I nod and say, "Yeah. That would be cool. Why don't you just . . . just stay at my place for a little bit until we can figure something out."

"Okay," he says.

We don't really say much the whole way to my house, and that's fine, because for knowing the dude almost my whole life, this is surprisingly awkward. I'm not actually sure if we've *ever* hung out completely alone, even in a driving-you-home capacity.

I don't have to give him directions to my place; he lives super close to me—it's right on his way—and he's been over enough times with his parents that he can figure it out up until the last couple streets. So it's legitimately silent.

I don't turn on the radio, even, because Ezra has got to be the literal most observant Reform Jew I have ever met. More than anyone in my family, way more than his parents, even. And I'm just assuming breaking a rule like no-radio-on-Shabbat in his car would irritate him. So I pull a few songs to the front of my mind and plunk my head against the window, until all the songs melt slowly into "Go the Distance" from *Hercules*—like almost every song always does eventually in my brain—and wait it out.

We pull up to my house and he follows me inside, hand on the back of his neck. Like he's nervous. Which is kind of funny, since I've basically only ever seen Ezra looking self-assured and borderline arrogant.

Ben cocks an eyebrow when Ezra comes in and shuts the door. Kaylee smiles at him *way* too brightly and says, "Hey, Ezra!" with an exclamation point in her voice. Like the small, adorable freshman she is. She's enthusiastic enough that even Ezra, who I assumed would be nothing but logical and analytical when it came to matters of the heart, half-smiles to himself. His ears get a little red.

Kaylee is as subtle as a Michael Bay movie.

He says, "Hey, Kaylee," and I pop into the kitchen to get us a couple Cokes before we crest the stairs to my room.

"So," I say when we get in there and shut the door, "any bright ideas?"

"Not that you haven't already shut down."

I shrug and pull out the notebook we were using in class and a pencil.

He glances at it, reaches for his own backpack, then freezes at the zipper. "Dammit."

"Guess I'm *taking point on the project* tonight then," I say, and I know my grin is a little more wicked than it should be. It's just that his lips purse so perfectly. His brow furrows so immediately and beautifully. I highly doubt he'll write on Shabbat unless he has to.

"This is already exhausting," he says.

I shrug. "I'll write legibly," I say.

"Sure."

He shifts so his knees press into his palms—literally sitting on his hands as I open my notebook to write. I'm not actually trying to be an asshole. Like I'm not doing some kind of "Haha, look at you, choosing to abide by rules that I do not" thing. I respect the guy. It's just that his face makes it impossible not to take just a *little* pleasure in knowing I get to be in charge of all of this tonight.

"Would you rather do this tomorrow night?" I offer, sincerely. "Or Sunday?"

He sighs. I am beginning to wonder if that's just the way he breathes. "No. It's fine."

"You sure you're cool with doing the work to brainstorm this on Shabbos? Or is that . . . a gray enough area for you?"

I'm going out of my way to be considerate, to make sure he doesn't feel pressured because I am a GOOD AND NICE PERSON, but his lips just tick. He says, dodging the question, "Let's just get this started. I'd like the weekend to start gathering research."

What that means is: *I would rather not, Amalia, but I absolutely cannot stand slacking off for another twenty-four hours and I'm not going to engage with it.*

"Of course you would." I kind of laugh, and I think maybe that will annoy him, but he just runs a hand back through his straight, dark hair, and laughs a little with me.

I raise an eyebrow.

"I'm capable of laughter, *Yaabez.*"

I'm so shocked at the playful inflection in his voice, it takes me a half-second to gather myself enough to laugh. But then I do. "Don't do that," I say, cracking up.

"Why not? You *Holtz* me all the time."

"That's filthy, Holtz."

He blushes immediately, just a little. His expression doesn't shift, but color crawls into his cheeks, light like watercolor.

I say, "Last-naming me sounds weird coming out of your mouth. That move is not for you."

Ezra rolls his eyes, cheeks and ears still pink, mouth still turned up at the corners.

"Now," I continue, "are you gonna give me some Shabbat provisions to break or am I just holding this pencil for no reason?"

A literal groan. Then, "I legitimately have nothing. You think everything I want to do is like . . . charting the drying time of cement."

"Well, whose fault is that?" My phone buzzes in my pocket. "One sec." I glance down at it. "Oh shit," I say. "Kaylee says you left your headlights on."

"Dammit, did I?" Ezra stands and says, "You don't think this is a ploy for her to start making out with me in the hallway?"

I bark out a laugh. "I don't know, man, leave my room at your own risk."

I'm still giggling about it thirty seconds after he's left. Poor Kaylee. She would actually die if she knew he'd said that; *I'm* about to die just out of surprise that he was observant enough to acknowledge it and cool enough to joke about something as plebeian as making out. Then I freeze.

Maybe that's it.

I've got it.

"Well," Ezra says when he comes back in, "no attack in the halls; my lights really were on so—"

"Ezra," I say.

He shuts his mouth and looks at me. Then sits on my gray carpet. Takes a drink of his Coke.

"I have it. Okay, listen, you're gonna wanna shut this down on instinct but don't."

He says, blithely, "No promises," and I ignore it.

"I was just sitting here, thinking about how shocked I was that you were an astute enough student of human nature that you would even recognize my sister's obvious, like, mating call down there—"

He literally chokes on his drink.

"—and I thought, what if we did an experiment on that?"

"On . . . me and your sister? Listen, I said no promises. I will *not*—"

"No," I say. "Lord. Holtz. No. On love. Like, on relationships. There was this study they did way back in the nineties." I scroll through my phone and wave it in his face. "Arthur Aron, looks like? Anyway, they matched up these total strangers and had them answer a bunch of questions, then like. Stare at each other. To see if they could use science to get people to fall in love."

"Huh," says Ezra. I have the sneaking suspicion that he's being more agreeable than he would have been otherwise because of the palpable relief at my not suggesting he hook up with Kaylee. Another psychological phenomenon to chew on.

"What if we recreated that experiment?"

Ezra frowns and confers mentally with my carpet, trying, no doubt, to decide if this is foolproof and logical enough. "I don't know that we can take his hypothesis, word-for-word, and regurgitate it."

I breathe out through my nose. "Dammit."

"No, wait, I'm not saying no."

My eyebrows rise.

He says, "We could add in a matchmaking component. Come up with several research-based determinants of romantic compatibility, and have students volunteer to be matched up, *and* do Aron's study. Personality plus intention."

"They could journal it," I say. "Or like, video diary, or whatever?"

"Yeah," he says. "And we can compare results at the end. Maybe three couples?"

"If we can get that many, sure," I say.

He smiles, genuinely. A wide, enthused thing. I get this little jolt of excitement at his approval and start scribbling.

"So what we need," I say, over the sound of graphite scaring across a page, "is to determine what we think, based on our own conjecture and the body of research supporting it, are primary factors of compatibility."

"Yes," he says.

"Like an expansion on what he already did. A modern update on"—I glance at my phone again and read—"The Experimental Generation of Interpersonal Closeness."

"Yes," says Ezra again. "Perfect. Okay, yes, I think this can actually work. Maybe we're not doomed."

"Well," I say, "don't seem so surprised."

He shrugs and tips his lips in this almost mischievous way that makes his eyes sparkle.

"Look at us," he says. "Being brilliant. Surviving being in a room together for more than eight seconds."

"Truly, a miracle."

Then the room falls silent. For a couple full minutes, at least.

"I, uh. Yeah, I should probably get back, actually," he says.

"Sure."

That's fine with me. Because it seems like we will in fact be capable of working together without committing murder, but that doesn't mean I want to spend the whole evening with him, being subtly chastised for breathing wrong.

"Let me walk you out," I say.

"You don't have to," he says, but I follow him out the door to his car anyway, notebook still in hand.

"Hold up just a sec," I say, and I rip the page out of my notebook. Then hand it to him.

He eyes it then me, then says, "Why are you giving me this?"

"Because you'll feel better knowing I'm not gonna lose it. And then I won't lose it and have to deal with you riding my ass about it on Tuesday."

He adjusts his glasses at me.

"Plus," I say, "now you can do what I know you're gonna be dying to do the second it hits like 8:30 tomorrow—"

He raises an eyebrow, playfully. As close to a smile as he usually gets. "8:47."

"Amazing. You actually have all the times memorized?"

A little exasperated tic in his jaw. He has a number of ways to show that specific emotion, I am learning.

"I have an app," he says. "I checked to see what time Shabbat ends like three hours ago."

He's a little defensive, but now I'm smiling instead when I say, "Well, hat's off." And I don't say it in a jerky sarcastic way. His jaw unclenches, the littlest bit. I continue, "Anyway, I know at 8:47, you're gonna be dying to write all that down in your perfect, precise handwriting, and get this beautifully organized outline going, and I am trying to facilitate that. Better for my grade."

He peers at me, then just folds it up in a flawlessly symmetrical square and slips it in his back pocket. He says, "Thank you."

I say, "Don't say I never did anything for you. Good Shabbos."

"Good Shabbos," he says, hand still in that back pocket when I walk away.

CHAPTER FIVE

Observation: If an object in motion stays in motion, and an object at rest stays at rest, I suppose that means that humans, down to a cellular level, are resistant to change. But the law of . . . what? Thermodynamics? No. Murphy's Law. That's not . . . Entropy. ENTROPY guarantees that everything, everything will.

What a racket.

Skylar's house is one of those houses that looks like it was transplanted here from another time. It's old and off-white with a wraparound porch and these green wooden shutters and a long driveway with weeping willows leading up the path. Spanish moss, rustling leaves blowing dangerously across the pavement in the fall, the whole nine. Every time I show up here—all the time—I find myself wondering if, this time, the place will be haunted.

In the seventh grade, Skylar played Bloody Mary in the old already-Stephen-King-looking bathroom, and I swear to god I didn't come back here for a month.

So far, no hauntings, but who's to say if that'll stick.

I ring the bell and spend the two minutes she takes to answer trying to peel my shirt off my skin for a half second of relief. North Carolina humidity means I am unsuccessful.

"You dork," she says. "You can come in without knocking. How many times have I told you that?"

"One time too few."

There was a time, summer between ninth and tenth grade, that I snuck into and out of Skylar's house over and over, knew the exact path to take to hop the fence and scale up to her window and avoid the motion lights—could do it in the pitch dark without stumbling. She snuck into mine, too.

But things change and they changed with us, and I guess I just . . . ring the doorbell now.

Skylar rolls her eyes and opens her door, and I follow her inside. "Ellie's upstairs," she says. "Hope that's cool."

"Yeah, no, of course."

Ellie and Skylar started dating a few weeks ago. Ellie and I have slacked our way through a couple classes here and there, and there is some kind of special bond to that, like a pact. So I've always liked her. Even if it's still just a little weird to watch her stick her tongue down my ex-girlfriend's throat.

Skylar tosses her perfect brown-black hair and I get this sudden wave of peony and vanilla as she walks up the stairs. Ellie, of the precious overbite, amazing coal black dreadlocks, and absolutely killer vibrato when she hits the high notes in every school musical/concert/whatever, is sitting cross-legged at the top of the stairs, waiting for us.

"Now it's a party," she says.

I smirk. "Please. I'm sure you guys had more than enough *party* to keep you entertained on your own."

She presses her hand to her chest. "Amalia, I am a *lady*." When she lets it fall back to the old hardwood, I spot an extremely fresh hickey where her palm was and my mouth turns up.

"Mmhmmm."

"We were *practicing*," says Skylar.

"Ah yeah, the all-important mouth exercises." I raise an eyebrow at her. "Hand exercises?"

Skylar holds up a finger. "One, I'm a bassist. Hand and finger exercises do matter. Two, we really were working on something. Listen."

She cocks her head toward her room and Ellie and I follow her in.

I sit on the hardwood floor and lean back on my palms as light filters through the window. It's more a little old attic than a real bedroom but it's extremely Skylar. The light picks up the dust so when Skylar kicks on her computer and joins the violin and cello in the recording with her massive upright bass, it feels almost magical.

The instrument is bigger than she is, but I've never doubted that she is in complete control over it. The bass doesn't overwhelm her, which is saying something.

She has that energy.

It's quiet, understated. Because Skylar is quiet and understated.

But it's quietly, understatedly like she could slide down into a bear pit at the zoo and the bears would defer right away. She chooses to use that talent on giant musical instruments.

Skylar plays and Ellie kind of rolls her eyes but opens her mouth to sing and god, they're good together. Ellie got into a different arts school than Skylar, but they both got in. It's incredible.

Ellie's deep alto and Skylar's bass fill the room and I don't even know the song; it's in a different language I could maybe recognize if I cared but I don't.

I'm mesmerized.

I'm fixated.

I'm . . . I'm furious.

I'm suddenly so mad and sad and each emotion is fueling the other until I can't tell which is which. Because I can't hear them without my counselor's voice stealing the main track, their music fading into the background.

FAILURE. FAILURE. FAILURE.

I'm so selfish, because I'm supposed to be listening to my friends, and I guess, as usual, it's just become all about me.

My fingers curl on the wood, and I'm so glad Skylar isn't looking at me because I never have been able to control my face. Some people have resting bitch face? I have Literally Always Bitch Face with a side of Cannot Mask My Emotions. Ever.

I should be supportive.

I should be looking for ways they can improve before the talent show this winter (four full months from now—but that's Skylar) and picking out everything incredible about their performance.

But I'm not, I can't.

Like always—like *always*—Skylar does something perfect, and she gets exactly what she wants, and I am left here on the floor of her attic feeling just.

Completely fucking useless.

The song ends and it's actual seconds before I realize they're looking at me and that I should probably say something.

"Amazing," I manage. "You guys work really well together. You're perfect."

I about choke on it.

"We've been working really hard," says Skylar.

Ellie says, "Please." Then elbows Skylar. "*I've* been kicking my own ass. Skylar practices for fourteen seconds and comes out playing like she's Julliard-trained."

"Ugh, whatever," says Skylar, but she says it with this grin on her face that isn't *trying* to be smug.

It is, though.

And now I'm just sick. Looking at them so lit up by their art together is just a reminder of this extremely, extremely fresh wound. Self-inflicted. One I haven't even been able to tell my best friend about for weeks because I can't stand the thought of her feeling sorry for me, or knowing—like I've always been afraid of—that's she's better than me.

She doesn't even have to try and she's better than me.

Ellie doesn't do anything but smile, because she doesn't know me like Skylar does.

Skylar cocks her head and opens her mouth, a perfect pout of dark red lipstick and seriousness.

I say, "Shit. Shit I completely forgot about something I promised my mom I'd do. I have to go."

It's been five minutes since I got here and I feel like a complete asshole, but my actual skin is itching.

I leave and I feel bad and I feel . . . well. I get in Ben's commandeered car and I feel like I always felt back when Skylar and I were dating.

Like I have been found wanting.

I don't even know by whom.

I'm in a supremely shitty mood when I get home and Ezra Holtz is sitting on my front step.

"What are you doing here?"

He raises an eyebrow and stands. "I texted. Like four times."

"Did I answer?"

He purses his lips, flashing from a surprising *I am insecure* to *I am disappointed*. Which puts us back in familiar territory, and I am just fine with that. He says, "I spent last night organizing our notes and I wanted to nail down our plan so we can turn it all in on Tuesday."

"It's Sunday, Holtz."

"What?" he says, looking around himself in fake shock. "For how long?"

I flip him off.

"Honestly, Amalia, we're partners and I came to work and—"

I scratch my head and my fingers get caught in my utterly untamable hair, which kind of hurts, so I huff out this breath and shove past him.

"What crawled up your ass?" he says.

I whirl around. "You. You're exhausting me."

"I've been here for all of two minutes."

"Well that was all it took."

He straightens his spine and looks down at me. Adjusts the stupid collar of his stupid button-down. "Why are you in an AP class if you're not interested in work? You've never been interested in doing *anything*."

I scoff. "Okay that's not fair. You know I'm really into—"

I was going to say art.

He finishes, condescending as fuck, "Weed?"

"Oh my god." I look up at the sky. "Oh my god, how did I think we were going to be able to work together? How am I supposed to walk away with any semblance of a grade when this project is about understanding humans, and the person I'm supposed to count on to do that is *you*?"

I don't know if he's about to laugh or yell at me, but this look spreads across his face that could go either way. "Sure," he says. "Yeah, I'm sure you're really concerned. About your grades."

"Because I'm just a complete waste of space, Ezra?"

He furrows his brow. "No. No that's not what I—"

"I'm just this inconvenient person you have to suffer through so you can tolerate class and synagogue and whatever, and if you had your way, you wouldn't descend to this altitude to speak to me."

"Amalia."

"Even if I tried, even if I cared, I'd bring you down."

He says, sharply, like a command, *"Amalia,"* and grabs me by the shoulders. Hard enough to pull me up out of this little ridiculous immature pity party. "What is going on?"

I say, "I care about things. I care about this grade."

"Okay," he says, letting go of me, but it's conciliatory. It's a gift, like he doesn't believe me. And for whatever reason, I need him to believe me. I need him not to give me validation like it's something to be given out for free.

Like Skylar would give me if I asked her to look at one of my paintings, which are apparently shit.

I say, "I *need* this grade."

He sighs and rubs this perma-furrow between his eyebrows. "Why?"

"Why do you need good grades, you pretentious ass?"

Another sigh, louder and through his nostrils. "Because I got a scholarship? To one of the top engineering schools in the country? Aren't you going to art school?"

I'm seeing red again, but I make myself breathe because I'm tired. I'm too tired to knock him over the head for assuming an engineering degree means something and artists are a joke. Of course he thinks that, of course Ezra Effing Holtz thinks a *lot* of maddening things.

I say, instead of throwing him into one of the support beams of this front porch, "No."

The second I say it, I hear it. I hear how it sounds. It sounds like I'm dying, it sounds like I have actually deflated while making the words come out. I heard it all confident and strong in my head, but when I said it, it . . . well. It sounded different. Like this was absolutely, positively, eight hundred percent not my choice.

"Oh," he says. Then, searching my face in a way that makes the air a little thick, makes me need to take a step backward: "*Oh.*"

"Don't," I say.

He puts up his hands. "I'm not doing anything."

The thing I appreciate the most, well, the only thing I appreciate at all from this entire interaction, is that when he continues, he does it without pity. He just says, voice all crisp and sharp and cool, "Then get your stuff and come with me to coffee. We're working."

I bristle at him telling me what I'm going to do. Bossing me around like that.

Especially feeling like this, like I'm going to come out of my skin in sad rage and this beyond irritating self-consciousness.

But he just stands there all expectant, and probably objectively correct, twirling his keys around his long fingers. Metal shadows on the veins in his hand.

And I . . . well. I get my stuff. And I go with him to coffee.

CHAPTER SIX

The Control Group (n.): A group designed to be
as close to the test group as possible, but not to be
experimentally tampered with.

e.g., Two random kids going for coffee, tolerating one
another, who have not been matched up by ANY
DEGREE OF COMPATIBILITY AT ALL, and
who are absolutely certain to prove that an exercise in
both matchmaking and intentional vulnerability is
MUCH more likely to result in a love connection.
The control group should make this hypothetical
experiment provable. Just SUPER provable.

Ezra's drink order is not surprising. He sits down at the
little corner back table with an Americano. Nothing but
espresso and water and a distinct lack of joy. Americanos
are *efficient*. I get a pumpkin spice latte with two extra
pumps of syrup and just flat-out dare him to make fun
of me for it.

I say, "The most boring drink on the menu; that sounds about right."

He doesn't respond in kind, which is good because I'm kind of in the mood to kick his ass. Maybe he can tell.

I open my mouth to say, "Well, show me what you got," but Ezra is already speaking.

"Do you remember—" He furrows his brow. "Sorry, were you saying something?"

"No," I say, burning off all my taste buds on this coffee while his sits, lid off, venting steam. "Go for it." Wow, I will never taste again. I refuse to choke or stop drinking, not while he's staring at me.

"Do you remember like, years ago, we were probably thirteen? Something like that. Our parents had seen us talking after shul a few times and my dad got this wild idea in his head—"

"Oh god, yes." I groan and Ezra's mouth twitches up briefly.

"And they invited your family over for dinner."

"Yessssss," I say. My head is in my hand now, partially because I'm embarrassed and partially because it's giving me the best excuse not to touch this coffee. I can't have him realizing I made a mistake and should have waited like he did.

"I was too young for your brothers to want much to do with me, and Dad and Tate were so freaking set on us hanging out that they kept pushing it, and within, what? An hour? Of us being forced together downstairs, you had smashed my tarantula's terrarium."

I bark out a laugh. "Oh my god, Ezra, I didn't mean to smash your terrarium."

"You hated Rosie."

"I didn't hate Rosie!" I'm laughing so hard now that I'm concerned people are going to get us kicked out for disturbing them. "I threw a pen at your head and you ducked, risking your spider's life in the process."

"A *pen*. Try again."

"Okay," I say, then I open my bag and pull one out.

He slowly raises one eyebrow. "It was a remote."

I choke. He's right.

"Sounds like a you problem," I say.

"It was a *you* problem when Rosie got out and wound up on your head."

I'm cackling. He's still allowing an eighth of a smile onto his face but that's like doubling over for Ezra. "What a nightmare."

"You really are," he says.

I wrinkle my nose and throw the pen at his head.

He catches it smoothly out of the air and says, "You done trying to kill me?"

"The day is young."

Ezra sets down the pen on his side of the table and puts the lid back on his drink. He slowly sips it.

"Well," I say, "are we going to get to work?"

"You're trying to get *me* on task. Black is white, up is down." He pulls his glasses up on his nose and slides his notebook out of his bag. When he's not looking at me, that means I'm only seeing him in profile, and holy shit.

His jaw is just a little sharper than I'd thought, strong lines and little veins when he clenches his teeth. He's got this surprising bump on his nose, so it isn't perfectly aligned like the rest of him; it looks . . . not like he was born with it, like it was broken. Hair that most parents would have forced him to cut just a couple weeks ago—a little too long in front, not perfectly managed like everything else about him. It always looks like that, I guess.

What I guess is that I've never noticed these things.

And now, how dare my hormones? How dare I notice, traitorously, how solid his grip looks on that notebook, how shockingly strong and long his fingers look? How the slim muscles in his arms shift when he turns back to face me, all business now, semblance of a smile erased from his face. How dare I notice that when he says, "Well?" there is the tiniest little chip in one of his front teeth.

Suddenly I can't swallow, and this? Is because I'm looking at *Ezra*? Ezra Freaking Holtz?

He spreads his fingers on the pages laid out in front of him and presses his hands into the table, stupid ridiculous veins rolling under his skin.

Jesus, what a problem.

I lean back in my chair to get a little distance. Clearly I'm still riding high on hormones from when I hung out with Asia again last night and I need to call her again or spend a little quality time with myself sometime in the extremely near future because absolutely *not*, I am not so hard up that I should be looking at Ezra all addled with lust.

"Compatibility," I squeak out. It's not like I have a super high, uber-femme voice, but I'm not proud of this: I squeak.

Ezra doesn't notice, or if he does, his face doesn't make it evident, so I take that for the gift it is.

"Right," he says. "So I have a few ideas about what goes into that: background, beliefs, religion, orientation . . ."

He launches into it, and I follow up with my own theories on what makes two people a match—and the sun travels over the sky and streams through the windows.

"Are you saying two people have to have the same religious beliefs to be compatible?"

Ezra groans for the nine billionth time. "No, I'm saying it doesn't *hurt* and I'm saying people building from the same ethical framework—"

"Wow, okay, so if you're saying *that* is any kind of guarantee just because people come from the same religion—"

"I am going to throw this pen at your head."

"I will duck and you will hit that barista."

He rakes a hand through his hair. It comes away all mussed, like he just rolled out of bed. "Can we agree that similar religious backgrounds, or having personal beliefs that facilitate interreligious dating, AND OR having similar general ethical and moral beliefs might have something to do with compatibility? For the purposes of science?"

I take a sip from my very cold latte and glance up at the ceiling, pondering. "Yeah, I think that's broad enough."

"And obviously orientation is going to matter a lot here."

"Both sexual and romantic."

"Yep," he says.

I lean over the counter to see what he's writing, because, true to form, I have been jotting down nothing. If he wants to get carpal tunnel, I will do him the favor of allowing it. "Change that," I say.

"Change what?"

"People don't need to have the *same* romantic or sexual orientations, they just need to have compatible ones."

"Oh, duh, yeah, you're right."

"WHOA," I say, too loud on purpose.

He jumps, actually drops his pen. "What?" he says, alarmed, staring at me.

"I'm *right*. Write that down."

It takes him a second to come down from the surprise high and then he rolls his eyes, extremely Robert Downey Jr. in *Iron Man*, and says, "Give me a little credit. I can admit when you're actually right."

"I can count on one hand the numbers of times this has ever happened."

He cocks his head at that, mouth ticking up, just a little, enough to tilt into maddening, then looks back down at the page.

"Ass," I say.

I can see the smile even when he isn't looking at me.

"This is pretty well figured out, I think. Now we just need to launch into these questions."

I open my mouth to respond and a baritone voice behind me hits me with, "Yaabez. Queen of silverware."

I spin halfway around in my chair to find Brent strutting up to me, toothpick in his mouth.

"I did kick your ass at that game."

"You wanted to *see* my ass. Oh, a lime green bra strap." He waggles his eyebrows. "That the same one from Thursday?"

"I'll never tell." I turn back to Ezra, who looks absolutely scandalized. "Please, it was Strip Spoons, you prude. He's with Sasha." I add, for Brent's benefit, "And he's not my type."

Brent says, hand clasped to his chest, "Right for the heart." He glances over at Ezra and says, "Edward, right?"

Ezra purses his lips. "Sure."

He turns back to me, like Ezra's not even there. Which, okay, Ezra's mood has darkened considerably so I'm not inclined to pay much attention to him either.

"You coming this weekend?"

"Whose house again?"

"Who cares?"

I shrug. "Good point. Figure it out and text me."

"If I do, you gonna come?"

"You'll find out."

He grins, big and goofy. "Bring that bra."

I flip him off and he leaves the coffee shop. Then I turn back to Ezra.

"So."

"Uh huh."

I narrow my eyes. "What?"

"Nothing."

"It's not nothing."

Ezra exhales through his nose. "It's nothing, Amalia."

I just lean back in the chair, arm flung over the back. I prop my feet up on the chair next to me, because I've never been able to sit properly in a chair, and wait.

"You a little booked up?" Ezra says, finally.

"I'm sorry?"

"You and your . . ." He waves his hand dismissively. "Social calendar. A little booked to be starting something like this?"

"Are you gonna rag on me for hanging out with jocks or did you want to work, Ezra?"

He scowls.

I hide mine.

Typical. He can't stand that I hang out with the party crowd, but everyone's known I do that since the eighth grade. Let him sit on his boring, quiet high horse. I don't care.

Ezra says, "Anyway. Where were we? Questions?"

I say, "Well, we could pretty much just use the stuff from Aron's original study, right? That's what we decided?"

"I mean, yeah," he says. "Or we could actually do work?"

"We've been working."

"Yeah. And I think we've made some excellent progress that I'd rather not phone in the last half of the game."

I narrow my eyes. "I'm not suggesting we *phone it in.*"

He snorts.

And just like that, in a flash, this shockingly easy, bantery rapport we have magically created over the last few hours completely disappears.

It's astounding how quickly comfort turns to anger, because yeah, I haven't proven anything to him yet, and yeah, I *am* coasting on almost no sleep in this study session because Asia and I hung out and fooled around just *way* too late last night, but that has nothing to do with us. Suggesting we use the original psychological study as framework isn't unreasonable, it isn't lazy. Coming from anyone else, he wouldn't think it was.

It's because it's me.

Suddenly I remember that this is how he is. This is how he's always been.

I remember why his beautiful jaw and incredible veins and strong hands and work-for-it smile don't matter. Ezra Holtz is a grade-A arrogant asshole.

I stand.

He frowns.

"Guess that does it for today," I say.

"Excuse me?"

"I'm done. I'm heading out. This has been fun. So. Bye."

I sling my bag over my shoulder and pick up my cold PSL, toss it in the recycling on the way out, and hold my breath for the impending shock of heat and humidity when I bust out the door.

I mostly hope he just sits there and doesn't come after me because, out of nowhere, I'm completely, utterly exhausted, and I don't really want to deal with him.

Of course, because it's what I want him to do, he doesn't.

I can hear fancy-shoed footsteps behind me, precise and intentional and measured.

"Amalia," he says, catching up to my pace with minimal effort.

"What?"

"We weren't done."

"Oh," I say, looking at him from the corner of my eye, not slowing down. Not stopping, which I know he would prefer me to do. "Well, I was done, so I think that effectively transfers to *we*. Feel free to not be done on your own, though."

"Were we not agreeing to move on to the next half of the project?"

I say, "I gave you my ideas for it, we disagreed, I'm leaving."

"Why?" he says, the first note of real exasperation creeping into his voice, rubbing it just a little hoarse.

"Because!" I say, and then I give him exactly what he wants. I stop. I whirl around. I throw my hands into the air and pay attention to him. "You can't go an hour without implying that I'm lazy and stupid and I am sick of it."

He reacts like I've just pushed him, recoiling. "When did I call you lazy? When did I say you were stupid?"

"I said *implying*, dumbass. Use that huge SAT brain."

"Alright, kettle, then let's talk."

"I'm sorry?"

"Do you prefer being the pot? Because the first thing you did when we sat down to coffee was tell me I was boring."

I feel myself flush and purse my lips. "Well."

"Let's not pretend I am not fully aware you think I'm some boring, uptight nerd who isn't worth your time."

"Okay, well, that's—"

"Always how you've felt about me. That's fine. I do think you're lazy. I don't think you're stupid; I *know* you're smart. But you're lazy and unmotivated and I don't trust you to hold my grade in your hands. You think I'm a cocky ass. Does that cover this?"

I blink.

"Come back with me to the coffee shop. Let's hash this out. Afterward, my dads would like to know if you're interested in coming over for dinner."

I breathe.

I breathe again.

I breathe just one more time.

Then I take his face in my hands. His pulse rises and I feel his cheeks heat, and mine spikes just a little being so close to the bones in his jaw. "Ezra," I say.

"Yeah?" He's shockingly breathless.

"I want you to really listen and take this in. Just, really make the effort to hear me here?"

"Y-yeah," he says.

"Take that pen you stole from me?"

A little furrow between his eyebrows.

"Go back home with it."

I lean in, close enough to his face to *hear* him swallow.

"And go fuck yourself."

I leave.

CHAPTER SEVEN

Observation: Catharsis is basically a purge. Like when hippies talk about ridding their body of toxins in a cleanse or whatever. Or like back a million years ago when they thought if you had cancer, the best choice was to drain the bad blood out of your body because that definitely didn't kill a crap ton of people. It was Aristotle who coined the term in a psychological, emotional sense. And what THAT dude meant by catharsis, I think, is, in modern colloquial English: A) Cry it out, bitch, and B) The sense of emotional release that occurs when you tell a boy to go fuck himself with a writing utensil.

I bypass the front door. I'm in such a crappy mood and I don't even know whose fault it is. I've been this way all day, I guess, so there's only so much I can logically blame on Ezra.

Well, screw logic.

I blame it all on Ezra.

Ezra Holtz with his stupid condescending smirk and stupid probably 5.0 and his stupid *future engineering degree* and his exceptionally stupid hand veins.

Lazy. That's what he called me, just right to my face. Like it was matter-of-fact, like any observer could have picked it out.

Amalia Yaabez: Brown hair. Five-foot-three. Olive-skinned. Crazy-haired. *Lazy.*

I keep my head down, praying my hair won't lure and trap any wasps, and make my way through the overgrowth that is my backyard. It's kind of a tiny little forest back here, oaks and sweetgums and mimosa trees. You have to really work to get back to the treehouse.

Dad and I built it one summer years ago, and my siblings will tell you they helped, but what they did was screw around and wreck a few two-by-fours and about knock Dad out of the tree for two months, and what I did, what *I* did, was work.

It's old. Ben is too old to care about things like treehouses, and Kaylee isn't really into the entire outside scene anymore, so we all just let it go sideways. It's not shiny and even and new like it used to be. One of the handholds up the side of this big old oak rotted off, so it's just a rusty nail, begging someone to get tetanus. I snagged my thigh on it once and I still have a scar.

I also still haven't moved the thing.

Kind of a lot of work.

I frown at that thought, *LAZY LAZY LAZY* flashing in my head, and climb up the old tree, pushing myself up off the nail with my toes.

I pull myself gracelessly into the treehouse, choking on dust and who knows what the heck else is up here. I should clean it, I guess. Probably.

I lie on my back, arms behind my head, and stare up at the ceiling.

My phone buzzes in my pocket.

Ezra: *I shouldn't have called you lazy.*

I roll my eyes and flip the phone over, let it lie silently there on the floor.

It sucks. It wouldn't suck so hard if I didn't . . . if what he said was just totally ridiculous. If he'd accused me of being overly emotional or something sexist and untrue.

But what he said, what he thinks of me—not that I care what Ezra, specifically, thinks of me—is the thing I've been quietly worried about since the ninth grade. Since I stopped being able to skate my way through all the gifted classes and realized I'd rather sit in the back and screw around when the teacher droned on about stuff I could do in my sleep. Since I realized that I wanted a *social life* instead of night after night buried in an organic chem textbook. Since my teachers stopped telling my parents how smart I was.

I've been in gifted and talented and all that since freaking elementary school, I've never had to study a day in my life, and high school, as it turned out, was a little different. People don't know this about me, that my report cards are usually at least bordering on decent. I can kill a test every time.

But homework. Studying. I've never had to do it before and I don't want to do it now, and sometimes I don't even think I know *how*, and it's all just. . . . Well, I guess I'm lazy then. I guess he's right.

I guess everyone's right.

Maybe if I had applied myself a little harder, I could have gotten the only thing I ever really wanted. The *only* thing. I was not the kid who changed her life plan nineteen times. I've never . . . I've never even considered an alternative. This—this was what I wanted enough to bust my ass and all my summer job money on art supplies and extra classes.

Maybe . . .

Maybe I could have had this whole life I've dreamed about since I was eight. Sliding into art classes, hands stained from oils and charcoal, hiding behind a messy bun and ratty hoodie, this cool, mysterious girl who stayed up too late drinking wine and working on a total modern masterpiece. A little studio apartment in the city scattered with all my paints, smelling like canvas, draped with sheets to protect the floor I'd ruined with color. After that, after I'd finally had enough living off Ramen and cold showers, a gallery. An exhibit with my name on it.

I'm Amalia, I'd tell people. *I'm an artist.*

I'm an artist.

Who the fuck am I if I'm not an artist?

Now I'm crying.

I can't even blame Ezra.

I'm crying because I know that's not true. That working harder wouldn't have gotten me that, that nothing could have, because when it comes down it, eighty percent of the time I guess I'm just *lazy*. And the other twenty?

The twenty that wanted this so bad she could taste it on her tongue? Isn't good enough.

That's it.

I'm not good enough.

And there is nothing, nothing, *nothing* I can do to change that.

By the time I am done with my total pity party, the sun has set. It was just this side of night before I sob-climbed my way up here, so it's not like I spent hours and hours up here crying in the dirt. Just like . . . hour and hour.

I breathe for a little while, and I climb down and take my phone, with its four unread text messages, which I leave unread.

In the house, Ben is watching *Bojack Horseman* and he looks up at me. "Molls, you've looked better."

"Shut up."

"Nah, I'm serious, you good?"

My mouth does one of those almost comically exaggerated frowns like little kids do before they're gonna cry.

"Shit," he says. "What's up?"

"Nothing," I say, running the heel of my hand preemptively over my eye. My mascara and eyeliner are probably all over my face.

But I didn't think ahead re: the crying this morning and didn't wear waterproof so it was probably already everywhere before the ill-advised eye rub.

Who cares. It's just Ben.

Ben hits pause on the TV and turns around, arms on the back of the couch. He just waits until I say something, which, as it turns out, is an astoundingly effective tactic.

I say, "Well I was hanging out with Ezra—"

"Yeah, I'd be crying, too."

I laugh. It's a little watery but it's a laugh. "He's not that bad."

Ben raises his big, need-to-be-hacked-at eyebrows.

"Okay," I say. "He is. But he just said some stuff I didn't want to hear and I'm being weird about it."

"What did he say?"

"That I was lazy." I shrug, like I don't care, like who gives a shit, this is Amalia you're talking to! Amalia Yaabez, who cuts class to go steal weed from the vice principal's glove compartment and light it up with her stoner friends in the woods off campus. Amalia Yaabez, who shows up to school, whenever she *feels like it*, in shredded jeans and an old ripped up leather jacket she found at a Goodwill, because it makes her feel like James Dean. Bad influence, wild, fun, rebel without a cause, Amalia Yaabez. Tell her she's lazy and she'll take it as a compliment! Who cares.

Ben narrows his eyes. I watch his chest expand, his big shoulders broaden. "Come here."

I groan but I listen.

Ben yanks me down onto the couch and puts his giant arm around my shoulders and says, "Ezra Holtz? Is a prick."

"Ben, come o—"

"He's a prick who doesn't know his ass from a hole in the ground and he doesn't know what he's talking about when it comes to you."

I'm quiet, way quieter than I think I'll be, when I say, "Maybe he does, though."

"You?" Ben pulls back and looks at me, really looks at me. My dirt-matted hair and my tear-streaked face, and I hate how vulnerable I am right now, but at least it's just my brother. No one else gets to see me like this, thank god. "You're not lazy. Look at your hands. They're perma-stained from all the art and crap you do all the time. You always smell like freaking turpentine and the rest of us have to retreat to our rooms to get away from it."

"Oh, gee, thanks."

"I'm saying look at you. You worked harder for that than I ever worked for anything."

"Like you didn't kill yourself at two-a-days."

"Yeah," he says. "But I never loved football like you love this. Like you love creating things. I was never hungry for it. You are."

Tears sting my eyes again. "Doesn't mean it's not lazy of me to do what I've done all through school. Just throw everything away. My potential."

He laughs, like straight up guffaws. I blink.

"Your *potential*. God, what are you, a mom?"

I narrow my eyes. "Don't be a butt."

"I'm serious! I've heard Mom and Dad use that shit on you so many times. You know how many fights I've gotten in with them over it?"

"Over . . . over me?"

"Yeah, over you, you twerp." He shoves me. "You're not lazy, you're just a smart kid."

That stings and I actually recoil. I don't want to hear that I'm smart; I'm so sick of hearing that I'm smart. It only makes me feel more like trash.

"I had to work my butt off to stay on the team all through school; you know that. Even as a kid. You remember they almost held me back in the second grade?"

"Yeah," I say.

"So like, I get to real school and I know what I'm supposed to do. I get Cs busting my ass and that's fine. 'Cause I'm not smart."

I sigh. "Ben, you're smar—"

"Don't bullshit me, Molls." He holds his hand out to stop me. "You, though, you're like the wunderkind, reading big books at four and five and whatever, probably in utero. YOUR FETUS CAN READ."

I laugh again, this time a little less watery.

"And you get the same grades I do, but you never had to put in the hours I did. Neither of us is useless, okay? Or lazy or whatever. You just . . . never had to do that shit like the rest of us and everyone told you you were gonna be the valedictorian and you were so damn brilliant and when you realized you could get what you wanted without giving up your social life like I had to just to play effing football, you did. But you're just so *smart* that when you get grades like me, like everyone else, you think you're a screw-up."

"I am a screw-up," I whisper.

"Molls."

"The only thing I ever really worked for. The only thing, Ben, you basically just said it. I didn't get."

"What else do you want?" he says.

"What?"

"What else. Do you want?"

I blink and sniff. I've never . . . I've never even really thought about it. I was so sure, so positive, wanted it so bad, that I just . . . I never even considered a Plan B. That I really could want anything else.

"I don't know," I say.

"Well," he says, "figure it out."

I swallow and look down at my stained, calloused, turpentine hands.

Ben takes a deep breath through his nose. "Jesus, you haven't even painted in the house today and you still smell like art. Figure it out in the bathroom or something; I can't even watch *Bojack* over that and my shirt is all wet."

"You are such a *jerk*," I say, shoving him hard enough that it should hurt but it probably doesn't what with all the natural muscle padding he's got going on in his pecs and everywhere. Benjamin Yaabez does not neglect his core.

"Yep," he says. He turns on the TV and I hop back over the couch, feeling light for some reason. Not like anything's changed.

It's just that . . . I don't know. I have a question. I have a problem to solve. I can stop wallowing, because I can't stand that for more than a few hours.

I just . . . have to figure out what I want, if what I can have isn't art school.

What do you want to do with your whole life, Amalia?

I just need one little answer.

Simple.

CHAPTER EIGHT

Hypothesis: If I want to start regaining some sense of control in my life, then I should consider starting with the tallest thing standing in my way.

Ezra Holtz is 6'1".

Ezra approaches me first thing Tuesday morning and, before he can speak, I hold out my hand and say, "Shut up."

He raises his eyebrows and blows out a breath, like he can't decide whether to be pissed or to listen to me or to be pissed but also listen to me.

"You were a jerk to me the other day and you made me cry and that's bad and you should feel bad." I almost regret telling him I cried the second it leaves my mouth. But also, screw him for making me cry; he should know.

He says, "Oh. Shit, Amalia, I'm honestly really sorr—"

"No," I say. "No, be quiet. Just continue being quiet."

He purses his lips and I see the telltale tick of annoyance in his mouth. The tiniest twitch in his upper lip. If he wasn't folding his arms over his chest, he would be adjusting his glasses at me.

"You don't get to tell me I'm lazy. I'll stop telling you that you're the most boring boy alive. We can think whatever we want about each other, but you are not going to be wrecking my grade with your assholiness."

"*Excuse* me? Me wreck *your* grade." His eyebrows are about even with his hairline, but to his credit, he stops himself. He runs his hand over his jaw and says. "Sorry. Go on."

"No, that's it. If you're done interrupting, we should get to work."

Ezra's face is stone. His jaw is clenched and his arms are frozen over his chest and his eyes are granite. He's processing, I guess.

Fine.

I sit at the desk and pull out my notebooks as though nothing out of the ordinary is happening, brush my absolute mop of hair out of my eyes and off my neck so it hangs over one of my shoulders. Then I primly start writing.

Cross out a line, adjust.

Cross, adjust.

Cross.

After I've ignored him for a solid thirty seconds, Ezra snorts.

I glance up.

He snorts again, stern mouth curling up in something that looks against his will. Then he halfway collapses into laughter.

A couple other kids are looking up from their desks and eventually even the teacher looks up and says, "Mr. Holtz."

"Yeah?" says Ezra, wiping tears from his eyes. "Yes. I mean, yes?"

"Something you'd like to share with the class?"

"No." He blows out a breath with tone so it comes out like an intentional, *Whew.* "It's nothing. I'm just—" And he loses it again.

I am dumbfounded.

"Honestly, Ezra," says Mr. Yeun, and Ezra just grabs the hall pass, doubled over laughing. Yanks it off the wall and leaves. Mr. Yeun looks at me from his desk at the front of the class and says, "Have you broken him?"

I say, "Well, I'm trying."

A couple snickers, and Mr. Yeun's mouth tips up, then he says, "No more outbursts. Get back to work. I need silence to grade these papers." He's not even making an effort to pretend he's grading; Mr. Yeun is reading what I'm pretty sure is a graphic novel.

I am working.

I have—because I *worked on it Monday, Ezra*—a whole application drawn up, ready to be critiqued, to let us create couples. It's this whole questionnaire based on compatibility from stuff like gender and sexual and romantic orientations to the littlest things like . . . like, "Who is your OTP? Who is your NOTP? Least favorite sandwich topping? If you were to be killed by a dinosaur in Jurassic Park, which one would you choose?" It's beautifully organized, if I do say so myself, and I go over it with a fine-toothed comb twice before Ezra walks back in, polished and confident and condescending once again.

"Ezra," I say when he sits beside me.

"Amalia."

"Have you recovered?"

"Yes," he says. "Thank you."

Mr. Yeun is looking at us with a wary eye, but we are being perfectly civil and Ezra doesn't seem to be in danger of imploding again, so soon enough, he goes back to *Ant-Man* or whatever it is he's reading.

"Am I just that hysterical?" I say.

"What?"

"Earlier. What the hell was that?"

"I, uh," he says. He glances down at the desk and rolls his palm over a pencil. It makes kind of a soothing noise when its edges hit the wood—one way, then the other. "Honestly, I have no idea."

I cock my eyebrow.

"This whole thing," he says. "It's got me a little out of my element and you just coming in here all hard ass and take-no-prisoners and the way you're like, verbally man-handling me. I don't know, it just, for some reason, struck me as funny."

My nose wrinkles and I glare up at him. "That seems a little sexist."

"No," he says. "No, not like that. Not that you're ridiculous. Just the look on your face, it was so completely dismissive. And I've—well, people don't talk to me that way and I think you know that and . . . you're funny, Amalia. I don't know. You're just—you're really funny. As it turns out."

Huh.

I say, "Oh." And suddenly I'm nervous. I'm nervous and a little unsteady and I don't know what to do with that. Or with the funny feeling in my throat and the hyper-sense in my skin so when Ezra's bare upper arm brushes mine, I literally jump. "Okay." That's all I can make my mouth do. Good lord, why am I so off-kilter?

"So," Ezra says. "What do you have there?"

"Compatibility."

He pulls it out from under my hands without asking, presumptuous, and gives it a once-over. "This looks good," he says.

"It does?" I mean to say, *It does.* But that's not how it comes out. I don't know what to do with this Ezra, the one giving me compliments and outright approval. It's weird. I don't know if I like it, but I do know it's weird.

"Yes," he says. "But I think asking faith and then religion is redundant."

"Oh crap," I say. "Yeah, that was an accident; I meant to only ask one of those."

"And you have some bizarre questions on here, but everything we talked about stayed so I think that's fine."

I furrow my brow a little, unsure if that was an insult or a neutral statement of fact, but I don't say anything.

Ezra says, "Velociraptor, by the way."

"What?"

"Velociraptor." He taps the page where I asked about which dinosaur you'd want to kill you.

"Ezra," I say. "Velociraptor? You're ALIVE when they start to EAT YOU. Have you not seen the film?"

He chuckles, then his lips twist a little and he laughs *exactly* like Ian Malcolm—that totally weird cackle. And I snort, and Mr. Yeun gives us a death glare.

Ezra says, "It wouldn't be a clean death. But if I'm going to be killed by an animal, I want it to be one that could reasonably outsmart me. That I can look back at as a ghost and not be ashamed that I was trampled by a stegosaurus or something."

"A worthy enemy is important to you."

"Yes," he says.

"Well," I say. "I go T-rex. At least you die in one bite."

"To each their own," he says. He mutters, "T-rex. You wuss."

I shove him and his pencil slips on his paper, so there's a lead line from the top to the bottom corner.

He narrows his eyes.

When we get back to work, I'm smiling.

CHAPTER NINE

Observation: There is a psychological phenomenon in which you write down anything enough times, or say it enough times, and it starts to look totally ridiculous to you. Even a completely normal, boring word. Plaid. Plaid. P-l-a-i-d. Plaid. Plaiiidddd. Plaid. Plaid. Plaid. It's the best pattern and now it looks bizarre.

Do something enough times, and it's ridiculous, but even if you know exactly what psychological trap you're falling into, well, Plaid is weird now. There's nothing you can do to immediately change it.

After my fourth detention session this week, I had planned a pretty epic evening of art-ing alone in my room. But the second I shut my door and set up a canvas, my stomach revolted. Like looking at a cup of vodka when you have a hangover.

I look at that canvas, smell the paint, run my hands over the brushes, and all I can see is what I don't get to have.

I can't do it, I just can't.

Not—not right now.

I flip my easel so it faces the wall, like that will ease the sickness in my gut, and quietly put away my paints and brushes.

I sit back on my bed and flip through a book that I can't really get my brain to fully process, pop in some headphones and listen to fourteen seconds of three separate songs, scroll through social media.

I'm floundering.

Apply to school. Create a portfolio. Select a major. All of these are things I can do, easily even. But the thing is, once you get over the intimidating decision paralysis of those things, you're done. You're supposed to be, at least. And now here I am again, in the Before phase. Wondering, and deciding, and ... I guess I should be researching schools again. Scrolling through majors, careers, planning a whole new future. I'm here in this awful limbo where I absolutely did not plan on ever being again, and I just don't know how to hack it.

So I don't.

I consider, for a moment, calling up one of my friends, seeing if there's anything going on tonight. A party somewhere, something I can crash and get the classic, *Ohhhhh Amalia's here! DO SOMETHING WILD! TURN EVERYTHING UP!* reaction when I walk in. My friends always love it when I show, and rarely remember to actually invite me, except as an afterthought. This weekend's invitation from Brent was a once-in-a-blue-moon kind of thing; usually if I get intentionally invited, it's more like what happened last Thursday. They remember me, not as a human to sit around and watch a movie with. Not as like, a *friend*. I mean, I'm their friend. They're my friends.

But it's not the same.

They—people, I guess, just in general—tend to view me as more of a walking, talking, cayenne pepper. I mean, it's fine; people have lives and everyone in the cool kid group has about a billion friends and I think everyone just assumes I'll show up if I want. I'll just magically know what's going on because I'm a magic pixie who knows all the Cool Shit going on in school. It's not an insult or anything.

It's not.

But the second I go to pull up a text chain, I stop. I can't handle them tonight. I can't handle my smoker friends either. And honestly, I couldn't go to a party even if I wanted; it's the beginning of the semester and if I'm slacking off *already*, there's no hope for me.

Besides, not that they're not my friends, but I just . . . I'm in such a crappy mood staring at this flipped easel that I really need to talk to someone who *knows* me.

I call Skylar.

"Hey hey, Picasso."

I smile and it's pathetically sad. "Hey."

"You okay?"

"Skylar."

"Yeah."

It's on the tip of my tongue. I almost open my mouth and say, *I'm dying because I don't know what I'm supposed to do with my life and maybe you can fix it. Tell me what to do.* But of course I don't. It's embarrassing. Plus it feels a little like a betrayal, having kept something like this from her for so long—not that I'm obligated to tell her everything about my life. But still. It's all too much to talk about so I say, instead, "What would you do if you couldn't be a musician?"

She's quiet for a minute. Then: "Well I have a couple back-up plans in place if that's what you mean. I'm realistic. Not many people get to be professional musicians; I know I might have to teach or work at a music store or something. Why?"

"Nothing," I say. "No reason."

She hums her skepticism through the phone. "You're nervous."

I sigh, regretting the call already. It's not Skylar's fault she doesn't get it; how could she? But I'm pre-emptively done with all of it. "No, that's not—"

"You always do this."

I frown. "Do what?"

"You spook," she says. "You're afraid to go to art school because you're afraid to actually take the leap and become an artist."

I cough out this half-offended noise. "I do *not* spook."

"Yes you do." I can *see* her say it. See her toss her hair and adjust her posture so she can look down her nose just a little. "Since I've known you."

"Okay, that's bullshit. Who was the *first person* to jump when we all went cave diving last summer? Or when you and Sasha and Brent were too scared to go on that ghost tour downtown? Or when—"

"No, Amalia, that's exactly it. You're absurdly brave when it comes to stuff like that. The immediate stuff. The adrenaline. All the things that make you edgy or whatever. But stuff like this? Stuff you *really* want? You back down."

I'm silent. I don't even know how to mount a defense without exposing my own secrets.

Sometimes, Skylar is a little too much for me. I don't know if that's the right way to put it. She's just . . . she's free with what she thinks, and she thinks a *lot*. Skylar is an introvert, and an observant one. She knows people in a way that I honestly never have and never will even though I'm the one who likes being around them. Who likes to do things and light up a group. Skylar, though, she's always watching, thinking, analyzing. And I hate it when she stabs right into me like this.

All the things that make you edgy or whatever.

Jesus Christ.

I like adrenaline and *people* and being the center of attention in a circle, and I like heavy artsy eyeliner and making out and weed and weird eccentric documentaries. I like finding cool, bizarre stuff (like ghost hunting, or the medieval torture museum or whatever) to pass the time instead of just cruising up and down the street. And that, what? Makes who I am less real? Makes everything I love nothing but a collection of things that make me edgy? I breathe in, I breathe out. I almost regret calling. But she's not trying to hurt me. If she knew I was already this wounded, she wouldn't have said this to me.

I am impenetrable.

People know they can always be honest with me.

I am *tough* and *cool* and I'm not so fragile that I can be hurt and that's refreshing, and of course it didn't hurt my feelings. Of course it didn't.

This is me we're talking about.

"It's . . ." Skylar exhales and it kind of sounds like it hurts. "It's exactly what happened when we broke up. I don't like talking about that and I'm over it and you're over it, I get it, but you spooked. I told you I loved you and you freaked."

That surprises me; she never talks about us. Not who we were when we first met. "That's not . . . Skylar."

"It's fine. It was two years ago." Her voice is a tiny bit hoarse and I don't know what to make of it. "It's just that you said it back. And I knew you wanted me as bad as I wanted you, or I thought you did. But then days later, we're just done."

"We weren't good for each other."

"I know," she says. "I get that now. Hell, I got it then. We're really different and we both exhausted each other when we were a couple, but that wasn't why you ended it. That's what I'm saying. You ended it because you spooked."

I breathe into the phone for a minute. She's not one hundred percent right. But she's not one hundred percent wrong either.

"Sky, I gotta go."

"Oh. Yeah, oh—okay."

I turn off my phone. I'll make it up to her later.

Skylar and I were a wreck. She is type-A, ambitious, over-achiever, serious. Bold. Confident. She might be an introvert, but she does well with people. They tire her, but she likes them.

And I am everything in the exact opposite direction. Being with Skylar, romantically, made me feel like a slacker. A jerk. A weirdo, like a vapor of a person. This cool shadow of a human who was there to liven up a situation and then disappear while she lived her important, non-weird, non-snarky, success of a life. Skylar didn't mean to, but she always made me feel like less. Like the lucky one.

Maybe that's bullcrap. Maybe it wasn't her making me feel that way, it was me. That's probably closer to the truth. It's probably wildly unfair to put that on her, because my brain is a jerk. But either way, that's how it was, and I did spook when I felt myself falling for her. Because it would have been a *disaster* in the long run.

We both know it.

Maybe she's right, though. Maybe it's because when it comes down to it, not only am I lazy, but I can't commit to anything.

I don't know.

Gracious, why is everything always at least a little painful?

I run my hand over my phone.

I punch in my passcode when it goes dark.

I call up Marisol, because Marisol has weed.

CHAPTER TEN

Chemical reaction (n.): The process by which one substance is transformed into another.

A similar phenomenon, known as the Yaabez Reaction, occurs when the substance of one's life is transformed into another, with or without a lead scientist's involvement.

"Dad," I say.

He grunts in response but doesn't really form human words. He's in the zone. My dad sculpts on the side, and he's never really made much money at it, but he *loves* it. He's good at it, too. Probably where I got it from.

Well, definitely where I got it from; it didn't come from my mom, who could not be more mathematically, unartistically-minded.

I pull up a chair at the kitchen table.

"Mom's gonna kill you."

"She's not gonna kill me."

I raise my eyebrows and look pointedly at the table, which, despite his best efforts to cover it in newspaper, is peppered with little bits of clay and who knows what other detritus. "I'm pretty sure I heard her threaten to divorce you if you ever sculpted in the kitchen again."

He smirks. "Was that what you heard? Or was she talking to you about your paints?"

"Mom can't divorce me."

"She can disown you."

"True."

He very intentionally continues his sculpting, hands coated in mud. Or what looks like mud. This has never been my forte; I've tried and everything comes out looking lumpy. Then again, my dad is terrible at painting, so who can predict what the art gods are going to bless you with? It doesn't matter the medium, though. The point is: we're artists.

Dad was the only one who really *got it* when I got denied to art school. He was the only one who could feel what I was feeling when all of that stabbed me in the gut. The only one who gets that art runs in your blood and it becomes all you can think about, everything you dream about. He works in wildlife management, and I just . . . I don't know how he does it. He loves it, I think, but how. *How* do you build a life around your second choice?

I grab a tiny lump of gray clay and twist it around in my hands.

"Foolish," he says. "Now you're implicated."

"You did this on purpose."

He says, "You think I would betray you?"

I narrow my eyes and he grins. Dad looks a little older than he is—a few more wrinkles at the edges of his eyes than a person would guess someone his age would have. A little grayer at the temples and flecked through his neatly trimmed beard (that Mom INSISTED he grow. I do not have any desire to know why). He's balding, too, but he's handsome. He's a handsome guy.

He says he's glad he's Jewish because the kippah he sometimes has reason to wear covers his bald spot.

I usually tell him to keep dreaming; they don't make kippot that big.

Then he grounds me.

Anyway, his eyes wrinkle when he smiles and it just makes him look older, like always, but that's also how you can tell it's real.

I say, "What are you making?"

He says, and I mouth it with him, "A golem."

"Again? You know how it went last time."

"What can I say?"

I poke at the clay. He eyes me.

"What's wrong, Ami?"

It turns out that there are a number of ways to turn *Amalia* into a nickname. If there is one thing I have learned on this earth, it's that. Behold the sage's wisdom.

I shrug. "Nothing."

He turns back to his clay and grunts again. It's a clear disagreement. I'm not sure I want to talk about it, really, but I'm positive I don't want to be quiet, don't want to be by myself. I need a human, and the human who won't tell me I live my life just to do things that make me edgy is my dad.

I sigh. Use my thumbs to press eye divots into my little clay ball. I run my nail over it to give it a scary little mouth. It's smiling. It's kind of cute, in a skeletal way.

"How do you do it, Dad?"

He glances at my weird little clay demon. "Well, I'm good at sculpting, Ami."

I roll my eyes and shove his arm. "No. I just . . . you work for the division of wildlife."

"Mmhmm."

"But you love art."

"Mmhmm."

"I just . . ." I blink down at the clay and squish it back into a ball. Then I roll it in my palms, over and over and over until it's smooth again. A perfect sphere. "How, Dad? How did you come to terms with knowing you couldn't do the thing you loved?"

His brow furrows. He picks up a little tool I never bothered to learn the name of because, like I said, I do not sculpt. It's like a paintbrush almost. But also, a tiny tiny torture device. A long skinny wooden stick with curved sharp metal on the end. He slices into the face he's sculpting, working on the nostrils. Then a little scar over the eyebrow.

"Who says you can only love one thing?" he says.

I grind my teeth together. It's not what I want to hear. What I want to hear is: *I regret it, my daughter. I wish I'd had the courage to try and try again, against all odds, and I have a magical solution for you that would have given me what I wanted when I was your age. If only I'd been smart enough to try it! I am a father and therefore wise and good at fixing all of your problems.* I say, "Art is what I love, Dad."

"So go to a state school. A regular college. Do art there."

"But I wanted to go to *art school*."

"We all want a lot of things."

I groan. "It's hard. Why is everything hard?"

He starts making the tiniest marks outside the scar. I can't even really see the difference on the surface of the clay. But he can.

He says, "You don't have to go somewhere prestigious to be an artist."

"To be in a gallery?"

"No."

I say, "It's not just that. I wasn't good enough to get into nine separate schools, Dad. Not even waitlisted. If that doesn't prove I should have some kind of backup, what does? How am I going to make it? I'm not good enough."

Dad actually chuckles, and then I'm annoyed. "What?" I say.

"Amalia, get a backup if you want a backup. Because maybe you're right. Making a living from art is hard. Not many people get to do it. I didn't do it. I found something else I loved, and I know it's impossible for you to imagine that managing the fish population at the lake gives me anywhere close to the satisfaction that art does, but it does. And that's not the worst thing in the world. To go to work doing one thing I love, and keep the other at home, just for me, that is what I want."

"So you're telling me to give up."

"I'm not telling you to give up. I'm telling you to find something else you love. Or something you like. Something you can see yourself doing in your life. And do that. And don't give up on your art; do both. Maybe you can be a painter; maybe you can get that life from the world. How do I know one way or the other?"

I rub my hand over my nose and streak it with clay. "I feel like my options are being decided for me. That someone else is making calls for my life."

"Sounds like life, kiddo."

"That's it?"

He stops. And he turns to me. "What do you want me to tell you? That you can do things exactly the way you pictured? You can't."

I recoil.

He sets his clay-coated hand on my shoulder. "I'm telling you what you know. That your dream was to do this one way, and now you have to do it another. That's not the worst news."

"It feels like it is." My eyes start to sting.

"No. The worst news, to me, would be watching you give up altogether. But I know you. You won't. Get the life you want even if it means taking a different route to get there. You can do that; I believe in you."

Now I want to cry but not so much because it hurts. It's an ache, not a gaping slash in my chest.

I want to cry because that is what I needed to hear. That someone . . . someone believes in me. There's no magic that is going to fix everything, that's going to make any of this easy, that's going to suddenly give me Skylar's life or fix the number of things that are wrong with me.

But.

My dad believes in me.

Even given the lack of useful advice today, that's something.

CHAPTER ELEVEN

Methodology: The most ideal set-up for a study is double-blind. Meaning, neither the scientists nor the participants know who is being manipulated and who isn't. Less chance for tampering when no one can tell what factors are at play. Theoretically, that leads to a cleaner experiment. Practically, well, sometimes it means no one has any real clue what's happening to them at all.

Tonight, Sunday night, I'm going to Ezra's. Partly because I haven't really gotten the chance to talk to his dads in forever, and I've always liked them. And partly (largely) because Ben was so content milling around the house and, after his show of goodwill the other day, I didn't want to dampen his day with "that tightass" showing up, so I did a secret act of kindness and offered to meet Ezra instead.

Ezra doesn't live too far from me. I have to map it— though, why did I? The guy meticulously typed out directions to his house that were better than Siri could have given me. Even though Maps exists. Sometimes, I swear, Ezra is like thirty years old.

Google, it turns out, does steer me wrong because there's construction on the route and I am immediately annoyed that I should have listened to his dumb instructions. Siri keeps telling me to make a U-turn—make a U-turn—make a—make—m—make a U-turn and eventually I shut it off in a road rage furor and find myself studying Ezra's directions.

And wouldn't you know it.

I end up at his front door.

He can never know.

Ezra's house is cute. It's not big and haunted like Skylar's, not cavernous like my grandparents' house. Maybe a tad bigger than mine, but older. Carpeted, dated kitchen, cozy little fireplace in the living room. It's one of those houses that, the second you walk in, you feel like you're in a *home*. I knock on the door and his Tate answers, huge smile on his big bearded face.

"Amalia Yaabez!"

"Yep." I smile, and my eyebrows jump up in this weird forced enthusiasm. Not that I'm pissed I'm here, just that I'm a little preemptively tired and that this is what my face does when I'm trying to communicate with adults.

"Come on in."

I do, and he shuts the door behind me. It smells like oranges and cinnamon and I think maybe I'll float along on it like one of those cartoons on a scent cloud. "Oh my god," I say. "It smells incredible."

Ezra's dad shouts from the kitchen: "New challah recipe. I'm trying it out before next Friday. Orange. Cinnamon. Chocolate."

I raise my voice a little and say back, "I'm obviously coming over."

He says, "Well, I'll set you a plate."

Ezra walks up the stairs and kind of awkwardly waves. "Hey."

I'm a little taken aback to see him like this—in a close-fitting T-shirt, jeans, bare feet. His hair is a little mussed, his shirt a tiny bit wrinkled. Like he's been—and this seems so impossible—relaxing.

"Uh," I say, "hey." I realize then that I am not just looking, I'm *staring* at his arms in that T-shirt. It's just that under a button-up, it's impossible to tell when someone is jacked. Not that Ezra is jacked, exactly, but that shirt is too small and it is ninety percent because of his biceps. Holy shit.

Now I'm staring again.

I clear my throat and take a step back so he can get to the kitchen and hopefully snag a little of that challah. I blink up at his face so I'll look a little less like a weirdo, and when he stands right next to his Tate and hones in on the challah, I realize I'm just going to start staring at his face now, there's no stopping it.

It's like changing the font in an essay when you edit it. The words stay the same, but the tiny shifts in perspective that come from moving from a sans serif to a serif all of a sudden alert you to things you hadn't seen before. The content is the same, but the context changes.

You can't help but pay attention.

Everything changes.

Seeing Ezra like this, well . . . I can't help but pay attention.

That little break in his otherwise perfect nose, I can't not look at it. Can't not wonder about it. The shift in his jaw every time his face changes expressions. He has his Tate's dark straight hair and his dad's thin, expressive mouth and jawline. People tend to think Dovid—his Tate—and Josiah—his dad—adopted him, but Josiah is trans, and they're both his biological parents. He looks like a solid 50/50, which basically means he looks exactly like whoever he's standing closest to.

I can see his and Josiah's identical mouths when Ezra says, "I was a little delayed—I was downstairs reinforcing the terrarium," and I roll my eyes and they both laugh.

"I'd apologize for Ezra," Dovid says, and then Josiah just laughs harder. Dovid cuts him a half-grinning look and says pointedly, "*and* my husband. But we both know it would do no good."

"I did almost kill that spider," I say.

"You did."

Josiah is still smirking when Ezra cocks his head downstairs, then stops and says, "Actually, you wanna go for a walk?"

I raise an eyebrow. "You're just afraid for your poor spider's life."

"Can you blame me?"

I groan and head for the front door. It's a rare day in September that the entire world isn't a sauna, so, sure. We can exist outside.

Ezra follows me out the door, hands in his pockets, and we walk together down his street. He makes a sharp turn a couple houses down from his, down this trail that veers off into the woods.

"If I didn't know you better," I say when the trees rise tall and close around us and Ezra eases into a slow lope, "I'd consider the possibility that you were luring me out into these woods to murder me."

He says, "Maybe you don't know me well *enough* if you think that's out of the question."

"Nah," I say. "I'm confident."

"Yeah? Even though you've proven yourself a possibly mortal threat to the thing I love the most in this world?"

I raise an eyebrow.

"Rosie," he says.

"God. I'll never live that down."

"And now I'm convinced you know me again."

I relax next to him, like I've been doing, bizarrely, this entire walk. Ezra is predictable and irritating, but he's familiar. I can relax into the calm, constant knowledge of him. We walk, him straight and tall like he's balancing a book on his head, me slouched, shoulders falling, hands in my useless holey pockets.

I say, "See, and that's how I know."

"Enlighten me."

"You'd hire out a murder. You're not the kind of guy who likes to get his hands dirty."

I quirk my lips up and steal a glance at him and his mouth twitches. "Is that so?"

"Call me a liar," I say. I pull my phone out and pretend to start recording him. "Tell me all about your murderous propensities. Careful. The NSA is listening."

"I'm not objecting to your accusation that I'd never murder you."

I laugh at the word *accusation*.

"I draw the line at my never getting my hands dirty."

I'm quiet at that.

"My hands live dirty."

And at that, I straight-up choke.

"You okay there?" he says.

"Yeah. Gnats or something." Great. Talk about *bugs in your mouth*.

He pulls one hand out of his pocket and flips it so his palm is facing me. And . . . shit, he's not lying. My throat knots up because what I see on his palms is dirt and callouses. Like intense, *how many hours has this guy spent in a weight room* callouses. "Probably got nothing on your painter's hands." He says it with this wry tilt in his voice, like he knows as he says it it's a lie.

I say, "I don't know, I'm half-impressed."

"Do mine ears deceive me?"

"Where did you get them?"

He walks a little faster so I have to push myself to keep up. "My hands? My dads. I hear it was a cooperative effort."

I roll my eyes. "The callouses, jerk."

He cocks his head, and behind those glasses, his eyes are sparkling. "I'll show you."

I follow him up the twisty trail which would fool a person, if they closed their eyes for long enough, into thinking they really were in the woods. The trees here are just so tall and thick and vibrant that the air smells alive. If you were dropped right here, you'd never know that just on the other side of the trees was road and cul-de-sac.

He veers off the path and I pause and furrow my brow.

"Thought you were edgy and up-for-anything, Yaabez."

I clear my throat. I just . . . for whatever reason, I don't feel the need to rag on him for last-naming me. I like it?

I say, "Yeah. Of course I am."

"Not like it's against the rules; there's no posted signs." We make our way across the kudzu. He says, "I'm still who I am; I wouldn't lead you across a protected vegetation area or something."

"No," I say in mock horror. "What kind of absolute *miscreant*."

He purses his lips. Runs his long fingers over his glasses frames. Then says, "There."

"What?"

"The rocks."

"I'm . . . not following."

"I boulder," he says and nods at a cluster of rocks up ahead, just a few feet from the concrete path really. It just, like everything else out here, feels more remote. "Climb with me. This is low stuff; if you fell you'd be fine."

"I wasn't worried," I say.

"Sure."

"Ezra. Don't be an asshole."

His lips thin, just for half a second. "Yeah. Alright, well. You gonna come up?"

He hops up on a low rock like it's nothing, like he's climbing a ladder. I have never bouldered in my life, but I'm not about to be outdone by Ezra Holtz of all people, so I clamber on up, too. "I thought we were supposed to be studying," I say.

Ezra says, from just above me on the rock, "And if you ever paid attention in class, you'd know we literally *just* learned that studies show physical activity can increase creativity."

I pull myself up the side of the rock and sit on top of the moss-speckled upper edge. Ezra keeps going. We're only one rock high, and that rock is only a couple feet tall. But I'm surprisingly wiped. My hands already hurt from the roughness of the stone.

"So we need to come up with our own updates to Aron's stuff," Ezra says. His voice comes out a little rough, a little *in the middle of something*. I flex my left hand across the spongy moss and grab my wrist with my right. Just to do something with my muscles and tendons and skin that will distract me from this unexpected uncomfortable awareness.

"The first set of questions is all about surface level stuff, right?" I say. "Weird little factoids that tell you more about a person than they should. So, I don't know, how about Myers-Briggs type?"

"Come on. No one knows their Myers-Briggs type."

"I bet you do," I say.

"ISTJ," he says without missing a beat.

"God, you nerd."

He shrugs and says, "You coming? Don't quit now, laz—" He stops himself with his tongue on the back of his teeth. "Don't quit yet."

"How about zodiac sign?" I say. I'm annoyed that I rise to the occasion but even the teasing implication that I'm lazy stings now. So I move.

"Please. Don't tell me you believe in that crap."

"Be more condescending." I pull myself, breathing harder than I'd like to admit, searching for a foothold to bring me up to the top of this rock that, all in all, will have me five whole feet in the air. I could have almost achieved this standing still.

"It's just meaningless, Amalia. My being a Taurus, you being a Scorpio, that doesn't say anything. Except that I was born on April twenty-seventh and you were born on November twenty-second. That has nothing to do with compatibility."

I hoist myself onto the stupid rock and blink. He's waiting there not even out of breath. I bet his palms aren't red and stinging either. He's used to this.

I'm not thinking about that, though.

I say, "You know my birthday?"

Ezra swallows hard. "I, uh." He glances up at nothing, and I'm so shocked to see him caught off-guard that I feel quite literally off-balance. He recovers from that single uncharacteristic stutter quickly, in a blink, really—back to cool and collected so fast I am pretty sure I made up the flash of insecurity. "Of course I do. I've got a head for dates, and I remember your bat mitzvah fell on Chanukah. Because you got totally insulted when I decided to give you a present and that present was a little eraser."

I cough out a laugh. I had completely forgotten about that. "I wasn't insulted!"

"Yeah, you were. You said, *Ezra. That's insulting.*"

"It was my birthday!"

"Well," he says, shrugging, "it was also Chanukah. Anything else felt extravagant."

"Code for: I was thirteen and I'd spent my allowance on video games or something."

He knocks my shoulder with his and warmth flares up my chest. "Give me a little credit. I'd spent it on a grow-your-own geode kit. Plus I never got the big deal about it; my parents had gotten you . . . I don't know. Something respectable."

"Which just made that dumb eraser *more* ridiculous. Because that was the one with your name on it."

He shrugs. "I wasn't going to take credit for my parents' purchase. Not for your birthday present."

I'm smiling and trying to move past this little tingle in my chest. This concoction of weirdness I don't know what to do with except sleep off.

Ezra says, "What about Harry Potter house? Everyone knows their house."

"Ooh. Okay, yeah. How about Harry Potter house. And . . . and best gift you've ever gotten. Or worst."

"One of us should have brought a pencil."

"Probably. I thought I could trust a nerd Ravenclaw."

He laughs and it lights up my chest. It's late, it's getting late. And I'm sleepy. That's why. I don't . . . lord, I don't know what's going on. "Well, I knew better than to trust a jock Gryffindor with academia."

I narrow my eyes and flip him off.

He half-smiles and says, "You want to climb more?"

I say, "Why?"

He furrows his brow. "This is way better than the gym."

"I hate the gym."

He furrows his brow even harder, staring at me, and I don't think it's that weird to hate the gym. Of course guys like Ezra, peak performance in everything, would believe in peak *bodily* performance and that probably means like, not skipping leg day and stuff which . . . I have lost my train of thought thinking about bodily performance because Ezra is standing there in that T-shirt that's tight and thin enough that I can actually *see* the outline of his pecs through it. And he's looking at me like he has never, ever looked at me, all intense and focused.

And I just . . . I don't know what the *hell* is happening here but I know I'd do just about whatever it was he wanted to do right now because of that stupid tight T-shirt. And then I'd regret it because it's Ezra, and not only do I not like Ezra, I can barely tolerate him.

But here I am, and who cares about my brain when it is not the thing doing my thinking for me right now.

Ezra leans in a little and I can smell the woodsy deodorant he chose, the very specific scent of dirt and rock on his calloused hands that are moving up toward my face.

What the hell what the hell—

"Amalia?" he says.

And I'm considering just honestly losing my mind and saying, *Screw it. We can't stand each other but there is no denying that you're hot, dude, let's get this out of our systems.*

"Yeah?" I say. My voice is all raspy.

"There's an orb weaver on your head."

"WHAT."

"Ssshh," he says. "Just. Don't move. Stand still."

"Oh my god," I say. I am completely frozen, and all my limbs are like . . . rigor mortising. This cannot be happening again. *Again* I'm with Ezra and a spider has found its way onto my head. What are the freaking odds? He's lying. He planned this. He's lying.

It moves and tickles my scalp.

"Oh my god, oh my god."

"It's fine." Ezra is focused on my hair. His dark brown eyes are intense and he's moving slowly, bracing himself probably.

"Get it *off*," I plead. I legitimately plead; my voice is hoarse. Spiders don't freak me out that bad but orb weavers are freaking huge. There's a picture of one on the internet actually eating a *bird*.

"I'm going to. It's not dangerous." He looks away from the spider to lock eyes with me. "Okay? It's not going to hurt you—"

"I know they're not poisonous, dumbass, but there's a sp—" It moves again, and I can feel it. I can feel it, holy lord. I whimper.

The second I do, something shifts in Ezra's eyes and he snatches it. Just moves like a whip and grabs it so quickly I can barely catch his arm moving.

One second the spider is on my head, and the next it's not.

"Okay," he says. "No big deal. You've survived this before."

"No big—" I start to get a little hysterical then clamp my mouth shut. "Nah. No big deal. It's just a spider."

His eyes dart over me, and he says, totally sincere, "You okay?"

"Jesus, Ezra." I'm frustrated and flustered and there's probably a million reasons but I can't get a solid handle on a single one so I just start climbing down the rock. "It was a spider. Again. Not a bear. I'm fine."

I hop down the rest of the way and cross my arms over the tattered leather vest that hangs around my chest.

"You gonna stay for dinner?" says Ezra from behind me.

I say, without turning around, "Obviously. We have work to do."

When Ezra catches up to me, his mouth isn't smiling. But his eyes are.

CHAPTER TWELVE

Uncontrolled variable (n.): Kool-Aid manning in to screw up your experiment. one pitcher-sized brick silhouette at a time.

Example: That stupid break in Ezra Holtz's stupid nose.

Tuesday morning, we have our pre-experiment presentation. What that means is, Ezra shows up looking like he's about to try a case in a court room, and I slide into class five minutes late, in the ripped jeans I wore yesterday and a Rage Against the Machine T-shirt. Ezra does not even try to disguise his frustration.

I don't know why it makes me smile.

What it *also* means is that Bill Nye here explains everything in pretentious science terms and I translate for the class.

"The participants will be selected this evening based on the most optimal factors of compatibility, using something of an algorithm—"

We'll match them up based on who we think will be into each other.

94

"The participants will be required to answer Aron's three sets of questions, increasing in intimacy with each set, and to log a number of hours with one another outside those sessions that demonstrate an optimal environment for—"

The couples will meet at least twice a week for the six weeks of the experiment, if possible. They'll answer some questions. Hopefully they like each other.

"A combination of dopamine, norepinephrine, and serotonin—"

Love.

"At the experiment's conclusion, participants agree to stare into one another's eyes for four minutes, based on conjecture that doing so triggers mirror neurons in the brain—"

The staring is weird, okay, but it really does do something in your brain that causes you to want to mirror the other person. To view them as deeply human. To empathize with them. So it's weird but it's important.

We lay out our parameters, the teacher approves it, and that afternoon we put out a notice on the school's little social media page that I feel like hardly anyone uses.

Fingers crossed I'm wrong.

MEET YOUR MATCH

Do you believe in love?

Do you believe in science?

Do you believe in helping out your friendly neighborhood matchmakers, toiling with you through this long torturous social experiment we call high school?

Let a couple PROFESSIONALS* match you
up with the future love of your life.
FOR SCIENCE.
(Please please please help us we need this
grade.)
*We are not professionals

We slap contact info on the bottom and post it online,
then print out copies to plaster through the halls and just
pray that someone, *anyone* responds.

Ezra is all keyed up about it—*someone* gets just a little too jazzed about academics—and he says we should
meet up after school, probably. To monitor responses. To
fine-tune the specifics. To really get started on the report
already, at least the introduction.

I say, "I can't."

He says, "Why not? Hot date?"

I say, "With Mr. Thompson."

He spits out his water. "I'm sorry?"

"Detention."

Ezra narrows his eyes and shifts the slightest bit closer
to me. "For how long?"

I shrug. "Just until the end of the week."

"Well that's perfect timing."

"Please. Our project's barely even started."

"How did you land two weeks' detention this early in
the semester?"

My hand goes to my hair and I glance at the ground.
Something about his scrutiny makes it a little hard to
keep eye contact. A little hard to breathe. "I just—I talked
back in class. Swore at him. He was being a jackass—"

"We have this huge project and your *mouth* landed you in detention already. Jesus, Amalia."

I try to protest.

He throws his hands in the air.

And leaves.

A

By the weekend, both our inboxes are flooded. I mean, flooded as in we have way more applicants than the six I predicted. We narrow it down to forty-five applications after several days of answering a billion asks for more details, and going back and forth with an exhausting number of people who can't decide/are thinking about it but it's kind of embarrassing/might be getting back with their boyfriend but like, maybe not, should I just apply anyway?

Ezra and I have managed to get things done, like I knew we would, despite Ezra's concern about my *attitude*, and here we are, sitting on my bedroom floor that I should have vacuumed, maybe, buried in paper. Rest in peace, entire forest. I wanted to go digital with everything but Ezra insisted we print off the applications. He had this whole tabbing and filing system worked out and when I started to nix it, it was like I'd suggested killing his dog. Well. Spider.

We've mapped out kids' political preferences, social strata, favorite TV shows, extra-curriculars. It's not like it's a blind study exactly, because we know people at this school. Both of us have gone here since the ninth grade. But we intentionally asked kids not to write their names at the tops of their applications so that, clues in their email addresses notwithstanding, we could be as neutral as possible when we matched them by their apps.

We are scientists, after all.

It's nearly eleven p.m. and we have two couples matched. We are, of course, arguing about the final.

"Ezra, I'm telling you. This is a perfect match on paper."

He rolls his eyes and leans back on his elbows, knee bent up, bare foot pressing into the carpet. "This? Is a perfect match? Look at the couples they both love in fiction. This guy loves Kaz and Inej. Han and Leia. Mr. and Mrs. Smith. She, however, has listed Steve Rogers and Bucky Barnes, Lara Jean Covey and Peter Kavinsky, Gomez and Morticia. Simon and Blue."

I shrug. "And?"

"And that means she wants romance. He wants . . . people who want to kill each other. It means they're incompatible."

"It means they both like to read. Both of them listed book couples."

He blows out a breath. "Beside *politics*, he just has: ANARCHY."

"She's a socialist."

"Exactly."

"No, they're both leftists, Ezra."

"Why are you so invested in this couple?"

I run my hand over my head. "I don't know, I just—I see it. Neither of them is religious, and they say that explicitly, which, in the South? Talk about common ground. They're both, uh . . ."—I scan the page, needing *something*—". . . straight."

98

"Well then in that case, let's just draw up wedding invitations. They're both straight."

I narrow my eyes. "I'm saying they have things in common."

"And I'm saying they're extremely different. She does cheer. He's a band kid who's in *debate*."

"Our first couple has eighteen billion things in common. They have *everything* in common. Are you saying people who have a few differences can't make it as a couple?"

Ezra pushes his glasses up and stretches a little, lengthens his torso and chest, and finally completely sinks down onto my floor. He looks up at the ceiling. "I don't know. Are you saying that they can?"

I say, "I don't know why not."

I crawl across the floor and sit next to him, where he lies, top of his head touching the bed frame. "You need to be more open-minded," I say. He groans and I flick his nose.

I don't know what possesses me to do that—to touch him. It's just a little bit of a mixed bag with Ezra. Being very deeply familiar and very extremely *not* all at the same time. I immediately want to take it back.

But he doesn't say anything that makes me feel like I overstepped. He just says, while looking at the ceiling, "You're going to match this couple and they're going to hate each other."

It's getting kind of late, which makes me feel like an old person—it's not even midnight. I settle down on the floor next to him, papers rustling at my feet. I grab a pillow and lie on my back, hair spread out just *everywhere* under me. "Because they're different?"

"Yes."

"And that doesn't make things interesting?" I glance at him and he turns his head over so he's looking right at me. I realize now how close our faces are.

Maybe he does, too.

Because he doesn't answer. He just . . . looks. Breathes. I am close enough to him that my breath is fogging up his glasses and I wonder if he'll move but he doesn't.

It's so quiet.

My brother's Irish punk filters up from his room downstairs through the floor of mine, and there are cicadas outside. The only thing that keeps this from being awkward. Or maybe it wouldn't be awkward no matter what, maybe I'm just being weird because Ezra is *so close* and he's *so*. He's so confident and hot.

I think I've always thought this? Well. Not always. I've known the guy since before his bar mitzvah, and I remember when he was nothing but limbs and braces, and when he wasn't being over-studious, he was being obnoxious. But since the guy hit puberty, of course I've known.

It's just that I've known in the same way you know that a wall is professionally painted. You walk by it over and over and think, "That's a pretty room," in the right lighting, but it's not like . . . well.

It's not like you're nose-to-nose at midnight on your bedroom floor.

I say, I *whisper*: "What happened to your nose?"

I watch him swallow. Watch him turn his whole body so he can fully face me, hip to the ground, resting his head in his hand. He looks comfortable.

What else is new; Ezra nearly always looks comfortable.

I feel like that is something that, up until this semester, people would have said about me. *Look at her, feet up on a desk, hair wild and who-gives-a-shit. Is there anywhere, anywhere that girl isn't just obscenely comfortable?*

Now, though, I am in academia—Ezra's world. And I feel like I'm constantly worrying, wondering, evaluating where I measure up.

And Ezra Holtz is lying in mine, and it looks like the most natural thing on the planet.

Ezra loosens the knot in his tie with one hand; his knuckles brush his throat.

"Why are you wearing that?" I say.

"What am I supposed to answer first?"

His hair slides over his eyebrow in a way that is shockingly devil-may-care for him.

I just sigh and roll my eyes.

"I had to give a speech in class today."

"Oh," I say. "Which class?"

"Speech," he says flatly. Adjust his glasses again; they're always slipping a little. "It had to be about current events. Mine was on whether the use of force is ever justified for political means."

"So you gave a speech about punching white supremacists."

"I did."

My eyebrows fly up. Ezra does not exactly seem like the punching type so I have some idea where he falls on this—

"I obviously spoke in favor."

I open my mouth. Close it again. Open it to croak out, "Oh." Jesus, he just gets hotter and I don't know what to do with it.

He taps that crooked break. "And this, nosy, I got from a fight."

I choke. "You're lying. Get out of my room."

He says, "You think?"

"How? Who? You're lying. I don't believe you."

"Eighth grade." His mouth turns up. "I wish I could tell you it was something cool and chivalrous but it was this guy—Rodney Baker—who'd been riding me all year. He was just a giant of a dude. The kind of guy who, the first day, you think might be the gym teacher and then he opens his mouth and you are certain you are wrong. The kind of guy you don't want to set his sights on you. I don't even remember what I did to get him to look at me wrong."

"Could have been anything," I say. I raise an eyebrow with pointed meaning.

"Come on. I wasn't that bad."

"Please. You and Mike and Moshe were a *nightmare* running around synagogue, and if I recall, Moshe went to school with us—"

I see the instant shift in his face when I refer to Moshe in the past tense, and for the second time tonight, want to take it back. "Shit. I'm—yeah, sorry. I didn't . . ."

"It's fine," he says. The quick pain vanishes and he's back to relaxed. Back to comfortable peace here on my bedroom floor. I don't know if it's real, but I know he means it when he says, "I like talking about him."

"You sure?"

"I'm sure. It's good."

I swallow hard. "Okay." It's a little painful for me to remember Moshe and he wasn't even my best friend. Anyway. Anyway . . .

I chew on my lip and look down at the carpet.

Ezra says, "I do take one issue with your statement. I was not a nightmare! I've never been a nightmare."

"You're still a nightmare," I say.

He flattens his mouth into a displeased line.

"And just because you follow the rules," I say, "doesn't mean you can't be a total delinquent."

"I'm sorry, I think it means exactly that."

His eyes are sparkling. *Sparkling.* Ezra Freaking Holtz is having fun.

With me.

And I . . . I'm having fun, too?

I say, "Yes. Yeah, it was totally fine when the youth group all came to my house and Moshe *somehow* hacked our smart speakers to play 'Never Gonna Give You Up' every time someone used the word *never.*"

"I had nothing to do with that." His mouth is twitching. Suddenly I need to see that quirk widen into a real whole smile.

"You're good with parents, Captain America."

"Is that a crime?"

"You totally distracted them so Moshe could get the job done and we had to unplug the system."

That twitch twitches harder and wider. I don't know if it's me or the memory of Moshe that's doing it, but I will take being part of that bittersweet cocktail.

"You did not," he says.

I shoot him a challenging look. "Yeah?" Then I stand and retrieve the skeleton of an old speaker from my underwear drawer. I slam it shut and feel this surge of victory when Ezra loses it. He almost chokes he's laughing so hard, and he has to wipe off his glasses then put them back on his face.

He rolls back over, hand on his chest, and says, "Oh my god," through laughter. "I'd forgotten about that." When he catches his breath, he says, "And you think I'm intolerable *now*."

I make a noise of disgust. "You were way worse in middle school."

"So what are you saying?" He cocks his head and smirks. "You like me more now?"

I furrow my brow and wrinkle my nose even though my pulse is going absolutely nuts in my throat. In my wrists. In my everywhere.

Ezra's eyes flick down for a second to my hands and catch there. Then it's like he realizes what he's doing and he looks back at my face. His own is a little red.

I look down at my wrist and say, "Oh god." When I pulled the speaker out, apparently a bra came out of the drawer with it. A little, like, shockingly lacy one with rainbows all over it.

"It's fine," Ezra says. He clears his throat.

"Good lord. Just. Finish your story. About the nose." Shit, I'm going to die.

I tuck my bra back into my underwear drawer and sink down to the floor right there. No way I'm risking getting close to his face again, not *now*.

He says, "Just that guy, he'd been messing with me all year—shoving me, screwing with my books, getting on me about my parents."

My hand digs into the carpet, on instinct. I'm immediately bizarrely protective.

"About them being gay at first, and then when he found out through someone, I don't know who, that Dad is trans, he kicked things up a notch and I just kind of lost my shit and—well. Wound up with a broken nose."

I say, through gritted teeth, "What an asshole."

"Eh," he says. He looks very self-satisfied when he says, "I knocked his tooth out."

"What?"

"That so hard to believe?"

"No, I just—yes. Yes, it is hard to believe."

I lean against my dresser and yawn.

Ezra says, from the floor, "What time is it?"

"12:19."

"I gotta get home," he says. "You know what—you win. Match them up."

"Yeah?"

He stands and stretches, that tie hanging loose around his neck, hair and face and eyes all looking adorably—alarmingly adorably—sleepy. "You've convinced me. They kill each other, though, it's on you."

"O-okay."

"I'm gonna head out."

"Think you can find the door?"

"Yeah," he says, "I think I'll make it."

He leaves, and I am exhausted and wired all at once.

I am twisted eighteen thousand different ways and he's probably completely fine and I'm so tired but damn. I lie in bed for . . . a while. Before I finally fall asleep.

CHAPTER THIRTEEN

TEST GROUP
PAIR A AND B

 INT: Wall, pale green. Low hum in background paired with bright edges of hokey wall décor suggests location as the computer lab. Camera flips to selfie mode.

VIEW: Location confirmed. In frame, Person A, a thin, dark-skinned Black girl with short, natural hair, two piercings in her right eyebrow, bright smile, just this side of embarrassed. She holds the camera in one hand, other resting on her lap. She sits in a sleek gray and black wheelchair, decorated on the sides and on sections of wheel in plaid washi or duct tape—difficult to tell which from video.

ENTER: Person B, a girl with long black hair down to her waist, winged eyeliner and subtle shimmer gold eyeshadow, medium brown skin. She is fat, face naturally siting in a position that suggests mischief, and in a plaid skirt that nearly perfectly matches Person A's wheelchair décor.

A's eyes pop a little when she notices B in the selfie camera, and she smiles, nose wrinkled, then sets the phone down in front of her and adjusts it so that it captures necessary angles.

A: "Person B, I presume."

B, biting her lip: "That's what my friends call me. Come here often?"

A, laughing: "No, actually, I've managed to escape computer classes up until now."

B: "If only we could all be so lucky. I'm Lina, by the way."

Lina holds out her hand and A takes it.

A: "Tell that to the camera. I'm Janelle."

Lina: "Camera, I'm Lina."

She raises her eyebrow at Janelle, who smirks.

Janelle: "Thank you. So we just got matched up, and I guess that means we're gonna fall in love."

Lina: "I'm pretty sure that's how relationships work, yes."

Janelle: "Well, it's science, Lina. Do I—I feel like I know you."

Lina, running her hand through her hair, leaning in toward Janelle just a little: "I think we had the same drama teacher freshman year?"

Lina blushes immediately and glances at the ground, body language shifting from open and confident to insecure. Closed, chin tipped down, arms folded over her chest. She glances back at Janelle.

Lina: "Which I am totally weird for remembering since it was like two years ago."

Janelle: "Nah. You're good. I remember now. We did some exercises together. I always thought you were cute."

Lina: "You did?"

Janelle: "Of course I did. I didn't say anything because . . . I don't know; it wasn't scientifically guaranteed to get me a half decent response. But anyway. Yeah. Shit, the camera; I forgot we were recording. You wanna . . ."

Janelle glances back at the camera, then at Lina again, a little catlike when she smiles.

Janelle: "You wanna roll on out of here?"

Lina, snorting: "Oh no, puns?"

Janelle: "Oh yes, puns."

Lina: *"Yeah, I'll buy you a drink and we'll fall madly in love over these introductory questions."*

Janelle: *"Sounds like a date."*

Janelle picks up the phone.

Janelle: *"This, you weirdo voyeurs, you do not get to see. We're gonna bounce."*

Lina, waving overenthusiastically, giant exaggerated smile on her face: "This totally isn't strange and uncomfortable at all!"

End recording.

⚗

It's been days and I can't stop thinking about Ezra. I can't stop thinking about us lying there on my bedroom floor, staring at each other and whispering like . . . well. Not like friends, exactly. Not like enemies, either, though; we've never been enemies.

We've been . . . different. Opposite enough to be irritating. To want to wring each other's necks. But it's not like I've ever hated him. It's not like if I had ever seen Rodney Baker screwing with him in the halls in the eighth grade, I would have walked on by. Especially *that* year. Of all the years to have screwed with Ezra.

I wouldn't have left him alone to handle it. I would have stepped in and kicked Rodney's ass before Ezra got the chance to.

But either way, not being enemies doesn't make us friends. We're *not* friends. I don't know how we could be, having next to nothing in common except a mutual not-exactly-hatred.

So it's something else, bubbling up in my chest, making it hard to sleep.

Is it slutty, I wonder, to be lying in bed on a Wednesday evening, daydreaming about kissing a dude you don't even *like*? Is it bad that I can't stop thinking about that break, that tiny nothing of a scar on his chin, the deep brown of his eyes or how resolutely strong his hands look? How they would look wrapped around me?

It's weird as hell to me, and it would be weird as hell to anyone else because how anyone makes the leap from Awkward Annoying Kid to suddenly Deadly Hot Annoying GUY is a mystery, but Ezra, by virtue of climbing a rock and lying on my carpet, has made it.

This is not a crush.

If he wrote me a note, I'd burn it.

If he called me on the phone, I would be puzzled, not butterfly-ridden.

If he . . . I don't know. Wanted to take me out to dinner and a movie, I would say no, laugh until I cried, then call him back just to say no again.

No. It's not a crush.

This, my friends, is good, old-fashioned lust.

My phone buzzes and I glance at it, half-hoping it's a worthwhile distraction, half-sure that basically nothing is going to qualify for that job. It does not. It's a group text from some of the smokers at school asking me if I'm ever gonna show up at the corner again and trying to figure out who among us has at least marginally decent weed, but no.

I'm not saying I'm never, ever gonna do it again. I'm not saying I didn't do it like, two weeks ago, being honest. It's just that now I really do have to show up for class sometimes. Not blazed.

I don't answer. I turn my phone off vibrate so I won't hear at all if I get any messages and I glance at my door to make sure it's locked.

It is, because I locked it the second I shut the door, because let's be real. I knew exactly what I was planning when I left the dinner table and couldn't get Ezra Holtz out of my head.

The lights are all off in the house and it's like 11:30 p.m. so hopefully everyone's asleep, but if they're not, well. Advantages to having an upstairs loft room away from everyone else means it's probably okay even if they're up. They probably won't hear.

At a certain point, I don't really care. I care about my hand slipping past the waistband of my underwear—which, why am I wearing these at this point? I kick them off. And I care about lazily messing around until I find that exact spot, the one I am so glad I took the time to find reliably so I didn't have to wait for any of the people I fooled around with to figure it out on their own.

I find that place and I think, self-consciously, about Ezra. Ezra and his perfect smile and those little scars that add interest to his face, the kind of scars I would like to draw. The kind of lines I would put on paper to perfect a piece.

I think about . . . his hands. The surprising callouses, the long strength in his fingers, the veins, I think about what his hands would feel like.

And *Jesus*.

I'm sweating. And I don't stop at one because why, what's the point of that? I go a little while longer because I'm allowed to be a little bit greedy, a little bit *slutty*, in my own bedroom.

I'm allowed to think about the exquisite failure of my art interlacing with the exquisite ridiculousness of lusting after Ezra all in one confusing masturbatory evening. I can think the word—*masturbatory*. I don't know how to think it in conjunction with Ezra Holtz without actually sighing disapprovingly at myself, but I can think it. I can take these things that aren't mine and jumble them all together in the one thing that is.

When I finally fall asleep, my heart is still beating a little fast, I'm still a little too hot.

And Ezra is still not out of my brain.

I'm actually mad at him when I see him Thursday. Not furious, just annoyed. At his collar buttoned up to his throat and his pleasant greeting face that isn't quite a smile. It's too confident, too condescending. Too . . . rehearsed, almost. Like he has a system in place for *smiling*.

Ezra glances up at the clock—I'm four minutes late to class. He just slowly raises an eyebrow at me then tips his mouth up, shuffling his papers.

Teacher's already lecturing; it's not a project day. So it's none of his business whether I'm on time. And honestly it's four minutes, *four minutes.*

I scowl and take my seat, then flip him off.

His eyebrows crease together.

Mr. Yeun pauses his lecture to say, "Amalia."

My head whirls around so I can look at him, and I immediately rake my hand back over my hair. As though that disguised it; I'm so damn smooth. "Yes?"

He purses his lips, tips his head at Ezra, then says, "Hands to yourself."

A couple snickers from the back of the classroom because that sounded way less appropriate than it should have, and when I glance back at Ezra, I'm blushing. I can feel it in my face. *Hands to yourself.*

God, get it together.

I can barely deal with this ridiculous irritation all through class, with my extremely close proximity to this boy who up until now has been barely a blip on my radar.

When class ends, I am grateful to the clock.

Ezra says, "Amalia," and I just walk out the door.

I don't . . . I don't exactly know what to do; all I know is that what I did last night did not rid this shocking, embarrassing tangle of thoughts from my brain as much as it cemented them there, and now I guess I'm the kind of person who doesn't know how to be in the same room as a boy.

Skylar meets me after class to whisk me away to lunch and says, "You look like you've had a morning."

"Well, Sky. I've had a morning."

She takes in my mop of hair, the flush on my skin, the probably dark circles under my eyes that say definitively that I am not sleeping especially well, and says, "Come off-campus. Tell me of your woes."

"I don't have woes, seriously. Just. A lot going on."

Skylar cocks her head. "What is it?"

I let out a breath. Glance up at the ceiling tiles in the hall. "It's nothing. Nothing I want to talk about, okay? Take me to food."

"Yeah." She frowns quickly, like a flash, then says, "Sure. Food. Okay."

And we go.

CHAPTER FOURTEEN

TEST GROUP
PAIR C AND D

The following is a text log between both Samuel Price (D) and me (C, Riley Greene).

Sam: So I guess we're doing this, then.

Riley: I guess so. Should we get down to business?

Sam: 😩😩😩

Riley: That's not what I meant.

Riley: I'm really doubting this decision already.

Sam: dude I'm messing with you, chill. We don't know each other. Shouldn't we like meet face to face to start this shit up?

Riley: I'd be much more comfortable getting the preliminaries out of the way digitally if you don't mind.

Sam: 😔😔😔

Sam: don't, don't, I'm messing with you again, I got you. You know me? Probably do.

Sam: That makes me sound like a cocky ass, it's just you know. Swim team and I feel like everyone at this school is obsessed with swim.

Riley: I know you.

Riley: Do you shave your legs?

Sam: well now who's being weird and PERSONAL, Ri.

Riley: Sorry.

Sam: gotta work on your sarcasm radar, my dude. Girl. Person. Well wait, is Riley a girl's name or a boy's name? I've been kind of operating under the assumption that you were a chick but I'm not like...against the idea if you aren't one. Don't let that get around if that's cool, I don't even know where I'm at with all of that.

Sam: that was a lot of information. Sorry.

Sam: guess it doesn't hurt to tell you I shave my legs.

Riley: It's neither name.

Sam: well that doesn't help me out a whole lot. I figure I should be allowed to know your gender?

Riley: No, I mean, I'm non-binary.

Sam: crap, obviously. Sorry.

Sam: I'm reading it over again and it's totally clear that's what you meant.

Sam: yeah, sorry.

Riley: Sam.

Sam: yeah?

Riley: You don't need to spend the next eighty-four years apologizing to me. Now you know. Is that gonna be cool with you?

Sam: Yes. I've only ever dated girls before but I wrote what I wrote on that app for a reason. So. Yeah.

Riley: well then. Maybe we should get some of these questions out of the way?

Sam: like this is an assignment or something lol bet you're on student council or some shit

Riley: no

Riley: . . . model U.N. lolol

Sam: THERE it is.

Sam: Have we gotten past some of this awkwardness? You cool to meet me in the hall after swim in two hours? Outside the pool?

Riley: actually. Yeah. Yeah I think I am.

Sam: sweet.

Riley: and sam?

Sam: yeah?

Riley: I think it's kind of cool you shave
your legs.

⚗

Skylar and I head over to this little hole-in-the-wall Indian place near campus. We used to come here all the time, but she's been busy with her girlfriend and with school, and I've been weird, so the combination has led to us not being recognized as regulars when we head inside. The host is new, which we would have known a few months ago. He gives us the same forced smile he probably gives all the high school kids who come in here for lunch and don't tip enough.

We make sure to tip enough. Always.

It twinges weirdly, like *this* is what makes me realize how little Sky and I have actually been hanging out lately. How weird everything feels with this gulf between us that she doesn't even know about.

We follow the guy to a two-person booth and neither of us need the menus to order, so we rattle everything off when our server runs over to take our orders. She, at least, is familiar. That settles my stomach somewhat.

"I've kind of been wanting to talk to you?" says Skylar. She's playing with the ends of her hair, which she only does when she's super nervous.

"What, uh, what's up?"

Suddenly that little anxious knot is back and I'm pressing my fingers into the table to calm down. There are no worse words in the dictionary than *I've been wanting to talk.*

"I feel bad. About the other night."

The knot untangles. I can breathe.

"Don't worry about it," I say. "Seriously, you're—"

"A bitch. I was being a bitch."

I roll my eyes. "Don't talk about my best friend that way."

She shakes her head. "No, I was being too harsh like I sometimes am and I should just . . . I shouldn't direct that at you. You should live your life the way you want to live it, okay? I know you're not just afraid to choose. You're gonna pick your school on your own time and go off and be a famous artist and leave me and my glamorless double-bass in the dust."

I groan. "Skylar."

"What?" She's smiling.

"Don't do that. Don't make your full-ride scholarship into nothing to make me feel better."

She sits up straight. "I'm not. I'm not trying to."

"I know," I say. "It's just . . . you don't need to do that, okay? I love you and I support you, and you and your upright bass could never, *never* be glamorless. Not with those wings." I tip my chin up at her eyeliner and her mouth curls up in a smile. "I was being weird and sensitive the other night."

"Stuff . . . just. Stuff going on," she says.

I can tell it's killing her not to ask, not to pry. Skylar is consistently an open book with me and Ellie, and then there's me. It's not that I hide what I'm feeling, I don't. It's just that I don't feel the need to blast every single thing about me at all times, and she tries extremely visibly hard to be cool about this.

But in her heart, she's not eight hundred percent cool about this.

I say, and it's only a half a lie—an omission, really, which isn't the same—"It's just. A boy?"

Her eyebrows pop up and she says, "Elaborate," just as our food gets here and we both have to spend the next five minutes shoveling it in to make sizeable enough dents that we have a prayer of making it back to school on time.

I shrug. "It's nothing serious. And by that I mean it's literally nothing. I don't even really like him, I just . . . can't stop thinking about kissing him? And . . . other redacted things."

Skylar's grin goes a little lopsided, a little *I see what you're saying*. She's always a bit scandalized by that part of my life, because as far as I know, she's never gone farther with anyone than she had with me—all above-the-waist stuff. She hasn't dated a ton of people, of any gender, but yeah, with the few she has—what I'm saying is Skylar has never had sex.

And I most definitely have.

"Who do you want to redacted-redacted?"

I scratch my head too vigorously, kind of wince. "Ezra Holtz?"

"Ezra Holtz—oh right yeah, valedictorian. Hot as *hell*. His glasses are . . ." She does a little chef's kiss. "And his arms, oh my go—wait. Don't you kind of hate him?"

"No," I say. "I don't. I don't hate him, we've just never gotten along that well. Honestly, it's not like I know him well enough to *hate* him."

"You just know him well enough that you want to redacted his redacted."

I choke as a boy on the baseball team walks by and mutters, "Which could mean she just met him eight minutes ago." I glance at him and see him mouth, with just enough hiss of breath that I can half-hear it: "*Sluuuuuttt.*"

"Excuse me?" I say.

He throws up his hands. George Edwards. *George.* Like he's ninety. He has two English monarch names put together in one deeply frat king concoction of Anglo-Saxon asshattery. "Nothing, Yaabez. I'm just saying, you ever wanna redacted my redacted, you have my number."

I do have his number. He's one of the unfortunate side effects of running around with the cool-ish crowd, and at least half of us feel this way about him, but no one will say anything about it because, I don't know, high school sucks?

I grind my teeth and stare at him. I want to come up with something cool, something that shows him I am Just So Unaffected.

Skylar comes up out of her chair. "Have a seat, you sentient can of Axe body spray. Maybe try not being such a dick?"

"And what would you know about dicks?" he says, narrowing his eyes. He glances over at me, then smirks at her. "How's your girlfriend?"

And heads out the door.

I clench my jaw and just stare at the table. That's a thing we get sometimes. Everyone knows we dated before we became friends. And everyone assumes we're still into each other; we have to be, right? But the thing is, sometimes people are friends and then decide to date. Sometimes people date, then realize they should be friends.

Skylar and I are allowed that. Not that anyone agrees, not that it's any of their business.

Especially with *me* involved, nah. No one is going to believe that.

"Amalia—"

"No," I say. "No, it's fine. You okay?"

Skylar shrugs. "He barely said anything to me. It's true, I know very little about dicks, all told."

I snort.

"Seriously," she says. "You sure you're fine? You want me to slash his tires or something?"

I take a huge bite of tikka masala. Way too huge since I cranked up the spice. I cough and my eyes start to water. "I think you want *me* to slash his tires," I say, gesturing with my fork.

"That does seem more in character for you."

I down half the cup of water in one go and clear my throat. "Don't worry about it, okay? It's fine. You should probably text your girlfriend and tell her we're not making out behind her back."

Skylar purses her lips. "Oh, yeah, I'm super concerned. She's very possessive and has no idea we're BFFs."

"Well," I say, "I'm just saying. Since I'm a complete slut."

Skylar makes an exasperated noise.

"No it's fine," I say. "Like I said. I'm fine."

We finish our food and drive back to the school.

I can't focus through my last two classes, can't get Jock Strap McLightBeer's taunting voice out of my head. He's an idiot, I know, and I don't usually care about this except that sometimes I care about this.

Sometimes, I care about it enough that when I'm flying solo thinking about a boy I don't like for his personality, it ruins things just a little, because I don't know how not to care at all if it's slutty.

I have a reputation.

For smoking more than I do, drinking way more than I do, having straight F's which, please. And wrapped up in that delightful little package of rumors is the rep I have for being a slut.

She lost it in the ninth grade. To a GIRL.

Okay, yeah, but summer between tenth and eleventh, she hooked up with a guy.

And in the ELEVENTH grade, she cheated on that guy with another guy.

A billion relationships in between, ended eleventh grade with some girl.

That girl

Is

A Slut.

What do you expect, she's bi.

Here is the thing. About this.

When people started spreading rumors about things you very definitely did not do, it's annoying. It can be a life-wrecker for a little while. But that stuff is easy to get past. At least, it is for me. I can say, "Well, screw you, I didn't do anything and there's nothing I can do to convince you so your disdain just makes you a jerk. Have a day."

The really complicated stuff comes when the rumors about you are true.

And in this one instance, I guess they are.

I've slept with people, more than one, and it's only the twelfth grade. I've done it before, and I've fooled around across the gender spectrum—just kissing and a little more here and there. To me, it was never a massive, huge deal like it is to a lot of people. I don't know how to make it a huge deal in my head, and at some point I stopped trying, so it's just *not*. It's something I *want*. But I know for Skylar, whenever she sleeps with someone, she's gonna call me and talk to me about every detail all night and rehash it over and over. She's waiting for someone she loves.

I think I'm supposed to want to do that, too. It's not like none of this ever meant anything, not like the fact that I've only ever done it with one person I loved (see: girl in the ninth grade) and it made everything else meaningless and empty or something. It's just that . . . I don't know. Kissing is fun. Other Stuff is fun. And when you're queer, suddenly sex means something different definition-wise than the sex-ed classes give you so it's a little hard to define anyway, but wow are people happy to do that for you.

I was too young. When I was fifteen. I feel pretty sure about that, at least for myself—really, we both were, wow. But now, I don't know. I know that I've had some stuff I would definitely call sex, some stuff I definitely wouldn't, and some I'm not a hundred percent sure about, and that whoever found out about it sure played a really accurate game of Grapevine.

And that, combined with the whole cheating thing in the eleventh grade—like we were married or something, like it was more than a guy I'd dated for three weeks—just gave everyone license to believe about me what they'd all wanted to believe about me since I came out as bisexual in the ninth grade: that I am greedy. That I am a *slut*. Never mind that Sky is just as bi as me and she's waiting until who knows when.

I don't think I am. A slut, I mean.

Usually.

I'm in my head about it sometimes, though, knowing how vastly and deeply my reputation precedes me, because like I said, it's easy to dismiss rumors based on lies.

The ones where people had all the information. Where they were given a certain set of facts about you and drew their conclusions based on real, true evidence. God, that's hard to shake.

Like if they, looking at all of this, have determined as a high school collective that I, Amalia Yaabez, am a slut, I don't know how to get rid of it completely.

I know I'm pissed that he's affected me like this. Some jerk I barely know.

I am still thinking about it, still trying not to let it get under my skin, which feels like admitting defeat. Feels like he—like they—have won. I'm still clenching my teeth and trying desperately to think of anything else when school ends and I shuffle past the AP chem classroom, just trying to keep my head down. Trying to pull my shit together.

Mr. Thompson stops me. Of course he does.

He says, deadpan, "I've been missing our traditional hour of total silence, Yaabez."

I sigh and glance at him. For one humiliating second, I think I might cry. But I shut my eyes, and when I open them again, I am cool. I am tough. I am *fine*.

I watch his face shift, the smallest bit. Watch him go from hardass jerk to wondering. He's seen it. The total stupid vulnerability on my face, and I hate it. This teacher, especially. I lock my jaw, just daring him to ask.

He narrows his eyes. Then he says, nonchalant, "You doing okay with this week's material?"

I grumble, "Yes."

"Yeah?"

I am silent. Trying to decide whether or not to lie. I want to. I want to go home. I want the quiet and not to be bothered. But on the other hand, I want . . . I want to get it. I want a distraction from all of this. I want—I hate this kind of, but the last couple weeks, I've been *interested* in this class. Despite Mr. Thompson continuing to be a jerk. I am interested in what makes up the universe.

But I just—I don't get it.

He's leaning against his classroom door, arms folded over his chest, looking at me in this uncharacteristically open way. Like he actually wants to help.

And maybe it's because I'm sick of rehashing everything from lunch, maybe it's because I've given up or something, but I say, "I guess—I guess I don't really get some of the stuff you were saying about reactions."

The tiniest hint of a smile turns his lips and he stands. He says, "Come in. Put on your goggles."

I can't help but smile back. The thought, suddenly, of learning. Of working on an experiment? Is exciting. I want it.

I follow him into the classroom. A couple kids file in for detention—Thompson's detention dance card is *always* full—but here I am. Voluntarily.

I put on goggles, and I actually listen, and for the next forty-nine minutes, I can do this.

For the next forty-nine, I am not Amalia The Slut. I am Amalia The Scientist.

CHAPTER FIFTEEN

TEST GROUP
PAIR E AND F

SUBJ. LINE: Study: Ariel Cade and Carlos Acevedo

SENDER: Ariel Cade

CONTENT OF E-MAIL: We met up two days ago at my house. That might seem strange but it turns out that Carlos and I have kind of known each other for years, because we've lived a few streets down from each other and have a few overlapping friends. Not well. Hopefully this doesn't throw off your experiment. I know him well enough to know that he's an anarchist who I never see without a Mountain Dew in his hand, but not well enough that either of us knew what superpower the other would be most interested in obtaining. Am I supposed to give the answers to those questions in these reports? Am I supposed to tell you that I've picked invisibility and I thought Carlos's answer (flying) was EXTREMELY dumb and unoriginal until he actually sat down and explained it all to me and now I almost want to change my answer? I don't think I have to tell you all of that, because then you might fall in love with US and then, there go your unbiased study results.

Either way. We met. We're only kind of sort of friends but not really. We'll see where it goes. He's pretty cute. So we've got that going for us.

Ezra says, "The correct answer to that question, by the way, is teleportation."

I roll my eyes. Not at the power choice, necessarily, but at Ezra's declaration of it.

I lean my head against the rock at my back and say, "Yawn."

"What do you mean, *yawn*?"

"I mean you're wrong."

"And boring."

I sit up straighter. "Your words, not mine."

He groans and eyes the rock I'm leaning against. "What's boring and wrong about teleportation?"

"It's uncreative."

"Who cares about creativity? It's pragmatic. You'd never be late anywhere. Your internet friends who live in all the corners of the universe, you could just blink and then you'd be having coffee. You'd never miss a class because of traffic."

I laugh out loud and it echoes off the rock. "I ask you what superpower you want and your answer is about missing class and traffic. Seriously, how old are you?"

"Well," he says, "what's your obviously superior choice?"

He takes a few steps to the left and strips off his shirt, in that single-armed over the back of the neck move that guys do. I literally choke on my latte.

Ezra glances at me and raises an eyebrow.

"Uh," I say. I want to continue with a freaking sonnet to his arm veins, oh my *god*. Instead, I finish with, "Telekinesis."

He rolls his eyes and finds a hold in the rock, then pulls himself up, muscles ticking below his skin—shifting and bunching and stretching out when he hoists himself up and reaches for the barest curve in the rock. I don't even know how he can hold himself up on it; it looks like nothing. Looks as smooth to me as the rest of it. But his fingers find some kind of purchase because he climbs higher, miraculously. He says down to me, "How is that better than teleportation?"

I lean back again, hair almost certainly wrecking itself on the rock in a mass of frizz. "Because it's more fun."

"That sounds right."

I blow out an exasperated breath at the implication. "It's also more applicable. If you can move things with your mind, then you can move yourself. You could make an argument for super-speed, flying, teleportation almost. Plus what if you could get down to the molecular level? Then you're basically a god."

"Hey," he says. "Look at you, thinking like a scientist."

"I could be a scientist," I say. Something about his tone, no different than usual really, rankles. *Something about his tone* pretty much always rankles, I guess.

"I'm sure you could."

He climbs a little higher, high enough now that I have to raise my voice to speak to him. "You sure you should be up that high? At a certain point, don't you need a harness?"

"Stand up," he says.

"Excuse me?"

"Stand up; I look higher than I am because you're sitting and looking straight up."

My nostrils flare at the command but I do stand. And yeah, he's right, he's not high at all, honestly. It's like those trick celebrity rock climbing videos on Instagram where suddenly you get the right perspective and no, they are not dangling off a cliff by one hand. They're climbing four feet above the ground. He's higher than that but he's not at risk of dying or something if he falls.

"Besides," he calls down, "since when were you so concerned about taking risks?"

"I'm not," I say. "I'm just not used to seeing *you* take them."

Ezra starts his descent and says, "What? You're worried for me?" And tilts his mouth in something close to a smile. Not quite, but just hovering there at the edge of his lips. Like something I could take from him if I really wanted it.

"No," I say. "I thought we'd covered this: you looked way higher up than you were. And I'm not interested in being labeled a murderer if you kill yourself out here. You and I both know our rabbi would have to rat me out to the investigators for having motive."

He does laugh at that. A low chuckle, muffled by a warm breeze and his movements down the rock.

"You and I have spent a strange amount of time talking about murder," he says.

"Maybe that should have been a question on the survey."

He hops down and picks his shirt up off the ground, then wipes his glasses off on it. He runs it over his face and chest to rid it of sweat and his face comes away a little dirt-streaked. It's the slightest bit red and he's breathing kind of hard. Sweat trickling down from behind his ear to his throat. His collarbone.

I'm watching it trail down his skin and my throat is actually going dry.

He watches me watching him. I can see it when his eyes darken, feel his attention shift, just the slightest bit. I blink away.

He says after a beat, "I don't even want to know exactly what question you mean. Don't elaborate. What is wrong with you?"

I laugh, harder than the joke deserves, and it's a massive release of tension, a bubble bursting so I can think. So I can exist in his proximity like a human. Not like a prehistoric cave person whose only drives consist of "Watch: boy lift heavy thing. Heavy thing: self. Watch boy have muscles, sweat. Top qualities in boy."

I glance up at him after I get myself under control and he isn't smiling—seriously when does he ever full-on *smile*—but his eyes are sparkling. The edges of his teeth are digging into his lip. I whisper, out loud, "Jesus."

"Hm?" he says.

I manage, "Let's get inside? I'm drowning in sweat."

And he follows me from my big rocky forested back-yard into the house.

A

The house feels . . . empty. Which is probably because it is. Ben's out most likely finding people to hit on (most likely scoring; who are we kidding? Dude is EXTREMELY popular with the ladies—gross), Kaylee is at a friend's for the rest of the day, and neither Mom nor Dad is back from work yet. They should be on their way any minute, but that doesn't make it feel less like we're behind closed doors by ourselves.

Now I feel like *Come inside* should have been overlaid with some cheesy music and capped off with, *Sailor.* Like I'm inviting him in for something different than study-ing. Or like he'll take it that way. That's a low-risk sce-nario because even if he did take it that way, and even if I didn't mean it that way—which, jury's out—well it's not like I couldn't say, "Whoa, buddy, I'm talking a *project* for *school,* back off."

He'd listen immediately.

I have quite literally zero doubt.

But god, why am I sweating?

Is it because I kind of want him to take it the wrong way?

Maybe—maybe I do.

Ezra says, after shutting the door behind him, "You mind if I get a glass of water?"

"No."

I don't look at him when I say it; I'm looking at the wall. I am fascinated by the paint job; by the barely noticeable texture in the drywall. The occasional fleck of peach pink you can see coming through the newer mint green, remnants from when my parents bought this place and the actual worst kitchen in the world.

It was sponge-painted—peach and aqua. Like, a literal round kitchen sponge. Just horrific. I think about that while the ice tumbles into Ezra's cup, when the water comes on and shuts off.

I don't think about what on earth has gotten into me that I am so aggressively trying not to think about what I'm trying not to think about.

"You guys redid your kitchen."

"Years ago."

"I didn't notice last time."

"Huh."

Ezra says, "Amalia."

I swallow and turn around. "Mmhmm."

"Are we going to talk about the other day, in class?"

I clench my teeth and lean up against the wall. Suddenly I'm embarrassed, halfway vulnerable which I hate, and I want something familiar and solid at my back. I say, "I don't know what you mean."

"Sure you do." He takes a drink. I watch his throat bob.

"I was having a bad day."

"I'd be willing to believe that. Except that it seems like you're doing it again. We're cool outside and then the second we step inside, you're weird and shut down."

"You're sure a charmer. Anyone ever tell you that, Holtz?"

He rolls his eyes and takes another drink.

"Seriously," I say, "next time you're trying to get in good with a girl, tell her she's weird and shut down. Works like magic."

He says, "I'm not trying to *get in good with you*."

"No?"

He drains the water. Sets the glass in the sink.

I roll my shoulders off the wall and head into the living room, then up the stairs.

"No," he says from just behind me. "I'm trying to get through this experiment with you."

"Then what does it matter if I'm weird and shut down?"

I can hear him groan, just a little, almost a growl in his chest. He's frustrated, and I don't know if I feel triumphant or regretful about it.

I open my door and Ezra follows me in.

"It matters," he says, "because we have to spend a lot of time together doing this and I'd rather be filling the time doing something other than having the shit annoyed out of me by you."

"Is that what I do?" I say. "Annoy the shit out of you?"

"Okay, if that's not something we've established by now . . ."

"No," I say, hands up. "That one's fair. And mutual."

His lips twitches upward, then pulls back down. He's still sweaty from outside, still dirt-streaked, and what a phenomenon. The ability to still be completely hot for a boy who's just told you that he spends the majority of your time together trying not to actively be too irritated with your existence.

That. *That* is what we should be studying.

Thoroughly.

He says, "Seriously, why the whole mercurial thing?"

"I'm not mercurial."

"You're mercurial."

"Shut up."

He snorts. "Fine, then, let's work. Get out your notebook."

"Well. I need to find it."

"You lost it?" he says, pressing his fingers to his forehead. He looks like he's in pain. I hope he *is* getting a migraine. I hope it just lays him out, because rarely do Ezra and I have things in common, but Other-Human-Induced-Headache is something we can bond over.

I say, raising my chin, "I misplaced it."

"No shit," he says. "It's a complete wreck in here."

My face flames hot. There are, in fact, clothes strewn over the floor and assignments, both new and old, hiding in various corners of the room, and there are a few mostly empty glasses and like two bowls and—okay but that's RUDE. It's not nice.

Ezra Holtz, as it turns out, giant shock of the century, is not nice.

I clench my jaw. "Jesus Christ, Ezra."

"What?" he says.

"Didn't your dads ever teach you to be nice to people?"

"I'm not interested in being nice to people. I'm interested in you finding your notebook."

"Oh. My god." Now it's my turn to rub my forehead, and maybe that's karma. Maybe it's just Ezra. Maybe I've been theologically wrong all along and hell IS real and it's right here, right now, in this bedroom. "I don't *have it right now*."

"Well," Ezra says, throwing up his hands, "then what do we do? You can't find any of your work because you lost it, and correct me if I'm wrong, but there is just no way you've already made a backup of your half of the work on your laptop."

I sniff and fold my arms. Glance down at the carpet.

"And you're not interested in us getting past this weird You Hate Me/You Don't Hate Me thing that I can't even begin to keep up with."

I huff out a noise and say, "Ezra, please. I don't hate you. I've never *hated* you. And it takes two to tango."

He runs his hand through that straight hair and it falls back a little haphazardly over his forehead. "I'm happy to admit to playing along here, okay? This is just like . . . the dynamic. But the other day in class you were legitimately mad at me; I could read it on you. And today in your kitchen, you're being weird again, and I get to deal with the question mark of that, and I hate question marks."

"Well, I'm sorry I can't help ease your discomfort."

His nostrils flare lightly. "Look. I'm not interested in being friends."

"That makes two of us."

"I'm interested in being cool enough, though, that we don't get distracted by interpersonal drama. This is distracting."

"Are you saying," I say, batting my eyelashes dramatically, "that I distract you, Ezra?"

"Yeah." He half-laughs. "Yeah, I am."

That makes me fall back half a step.

He says, "You and your annoying attitude and your completely out of control hair and your—I don't know, you're impossible to manage, Amalia. I don't know how to even begin to get a handle on you and so you're consistently exhausting and consistently distracting."

"Because of my out-of-control hair."

He lets out a breath. "That one I actually wasn't intending to say. But I'm a little turned around right now."

"You hate my hair."

"I like your hair."

I run my teeth over my lip. Ezra's hands are on his hips, sweat dark over his collar. He says, a little ruffled, a little stuttery in a way I'm not used to, "I'm not sure how we got here in the conversation. But I intended to come here and work, and all I'm trying to do is get us to a point where we can do that. So. Logically, maybe what we should do is set some ground rules. Lay out a map for how this is going to function. Without—without distractions." He swallows hard when his voice goes a little rough on that last word and I can practically *feel* my pupils dilate. Because I know. I know exactly what that roughness means. Exactly what he's trying to avoid by glancing up at the corner of the room and busying his hand with his hair again.

I snort.

He narrows his eyes. "What?"

"Just you," I say, stepping a little closer to him. He raises his chin and looks down on me. "You. And your rules and your logic."

He says, "Rules and logic are the only way the world turns. Without definites, nothing functions."

"God," I say. I almost laugh. "You're such an intellectual tightass."

He stares right at my eyes, brushes a look over my lips and back up. His eyebrow tics, just enough to tell that I've hit a mark. That's he's irritated.

I say, "I bet kissing you would be like kissing Alexa."

A muscle in his jaw twitches and he shifts closer to me. "And what have you been thinking about besides my mouth?"

My breath is hitched when I inhale and he hasn't even touched me. When I breathe out again, it's pitched. A little too high, a little desperate.

"Shit," Ezra says and he's almost laughing.

That's when he kisses me.

It's not tentative, it's not a question mark, but of course it isn't; Ezra hates question marks.

His hand is curled in my hair at the base of my neck, the other poised around my jaw and when his tongue slides into my mouth, it feels like an inevitability. It feels like an answer we've been working toward for a while.

He kicks my bedroom door shut, then slides over and leans against it, hands on me, a little rougher textured, even, than I imagined them, and holy *lord*, he kisses like he means it. Like he's done it way more times than I would have guessed.

I run my hands up to his shoulders, up his neck, sweat dampening my fingertips, heart pounding so hard in my chest, pulse racing in my throat. The fingers pressing into my jaw slide down my throat, over the curve of my shoulder, skim my waist. I'm breathless.

"Ezra," I say.

"Yeah. Yeah I know. What—what are we doing?"

I shrug; his hand is still on my waist. I'm still touching his biceps. "Something stupid?"

"I don't know," he says. He's breathing hard and it's an incredible boost for my ego. "Two people who don't even really like each other. Throw them together. Let them make out. Feels almost like an experiment." He raises an eyebrow. And says, "Logically."

I repeat, "Logically. It's a mystery, kind of."

"From where I'm standing."

"So we should—we probably shouldn't stop. We should probably just? Keep doing this?"

Ezra slides his fingers back over my ear, through my hair, and whispers into my mouth, "Yeah. For science."

CHAPTER SIXTEEN

Methodology: Arguably, the most important step in the scientific method is testing.

Over. And over. And over. Otherwise your whole experiment is useless.

It's important to conduct as many as possible.

RIGOROUSLY.

It is the first night of Rosh Hashanah, the Jewish New Year, which means Dad has been fighting for several days with the principal to excuse me from school on Monday because Rosh Hashanah isn't *a federally recognized holiday,* which means it's not the same as Christmas or Thanksgiving or whatever. No big deal, it's just the NEW YEAR and the start of the high holidays. And we will have this fight again (like we do every year) on Yom Kippur next week when Dad has to get me excused despite the fact that *didn't we just have our big holiday last week? She'll have Chanukah off, isn't that like your Christmas?*

1. No. No it's not.
2. Yom Kippur is the holiest day of the year. I'm gonna need it off so I can go starve to death in synagogue, not throw a party, dude.
3. Fine, don't excuse me. I'm taking the stupid days off.

It's a little exhausting, honestly, but we can't afford tuition for a Jewish day school so here we are. I got the days off after Dad about busted a vein in his neck, but I still have to make up all the work I'll miss. Which means, basically, that Mom and Dad and Ben and Kaylee are in the kitchen making fish and pumpkin and mansanada—a million things that are making my mouth water—and I'm holed away in my room studying chemistry.

Kill me.

This—*this* is why I never got straight A's. This is why I'm not fighting it out for valedictorian like Ezra is. Because studying sucks and it eats into so many things I'd rather be doing. I sigh and recalculate this molar equation that I probably could have gotten mostly done while the teacher was lecturing in class.

Kids don't have to do this crap on Christmas Eve.

But whatever, it's fine, I'm not bitter.

At least it's chemistry, which is a sentence I never thought I'd say. But I kind of love it. There's an artistry to it, or maybe that's just because of how colorful some of the chemicals are. But really, there's a deep creativity to scientists, I've learned. You're playing with the fundamentals of the universe, seeing what you can create, how you can rearrange the whole composition of the *world* to make things out of nothing.

I feel like such a nerd, but that's kickass.

If it weren't a holiday, I'd really be enjoying doing science-math. What the actual heck.

My phone buzzes beside me and I studiously ignore it in favor of molecular balancing. Skylar and her girlfriend are gonna be here in like an hour for dinner and I absolutely refuse to be late for that because of school.

Doing a fancy dinner is really common, but because we're Sephardic, my family does a full-on Seder. It's like . . . extra special, extra fancy, so so much food. Skylar doesn't miss it if she can help it because I do want to brag: my, like, entire family can cook.

Every single one of us.

My stomach growls and then so does my mouth and I frown and get back to chemistry. Think about science. About everything carbon-based, which includes food. Food molecules, scent molecules, filling the house and my nostrils—god, this is hopeless.

I groan.

And reach for my phone to distract me for five seconds. I need something to keep me in here because if I walk down those stairs I will get sucked into that kitchen and never return.

It's . . . Ezra. My stomach flip-flops.

Ezra: L'shanah tovah.

I scrape my teeth over my lip. I'm not really sure how to answer. I mean, I know how to answer. I've been responding to "Have a good year" since I could talk; it's just a repetition. But I don't know how to respond to *him.*

I haven't seen Ezra since our little clandestine make out session in my bedroom Thursday, and I'm so nervous about even talking to him now that I just blink at my phone. This is not, for the record, how I usually am about things like this.

Well. That's a little untrue.

I'm not completely badass about it, I'm human. I get nervous and stuff. But the whole *OH LORD WHAT NOW WHAT DO I DO HOW DO I ACT NOW AAAAAHHHH* thing is not usually me. Not since like tenth grade. The thing is, though, usually with people I kiss, they're a known quantity. It's the prelude to a (likely very temporary) dating scenario or we've already been dating for a few weeks or it's understood to be a one-time thing because we don't actually know each other that well; we just kind of got bored waiting for our friends who were making out outside and thought, *Hey, what the hell.*

With Ezra though, well, I don't actually know what we are. I don't know what he expects. I don't know what I expect. I don't even know what I want except that I do kind of want to kiss him again, like a complete idiot, and I don't want to date him because wow are we not candidates for falling madly in love.

So, where does that even put us? We're not together. I don't think it was necessarily a one-time thing, based on the whole *WE SHOULD KEEP DOING THIS FOR SCIENCE* thing? We're not exactly friends with benefits, though; we're more just like . . . benefits.

I don't know why everything is complicated.

I do know that my stomach is still tight, and that it makes me feel just a little bit slutty thinking about things in these terms, because I don't think everybody does this kind of thing. Which I guess is my M.O.

Also though, there's nothing *scandalous* or *slutty* about "Happy New Year, dude!" Like honestly, I need to get it together.

I text back, finally:

Amalia: L'shanah tovah, Ezra

He writes almost immediately:

Ezra: Tell me what you're eating. Different stuff than we are, probably?

I smile, despite myself. Like he really is my friend. My boyfriend. My I Don't Know What But Something. My Benefits. That's it. My Benefits. And send:

Amalia: Come over and find out.

I immediately hear the implication in my own tone and almost want to erase it but kind of don't.

It's too late, anyway, what's done is done and I don't feel bad.

My phone buzzes again.

Ezra: Can't. We're having dinner in an hour. Dad's challah smells INCREDIBLE.

I run my hand back through my hair and furrow my brow. I'm not sure what to do with all of this; this conversation feels too . . . too friendly? Too unlike the lead-up to

145

anything untoward? It's weird and I don't know what to think about texting Ezra about his dad's challah.

So I chew a hole in my own lip and write back:

Amalia: So come after dinner.
Ezra: I doubt I'm allowed to leave the
      house that late.
Amalia: Who said anything about allowed.

I smirk, imaging what he looks like on the other side of the screen. Affronted, probably. Insulted by my astute observation. He's probably adjusting his glasses at the screen, wishing it were me, wishing he could give me a proper dressing-down. My pulse spikes when he writes back.

Ezra: You know kissing at midnight isn't a
      thing for OUR New Year.
Amalia: Well.
Amalia: Maybe it should be.

I am feeling bold and nervous all at once. He could very well have decided that the kiss in my room was a weird moment of weakness and hormones and be regretting it right this very second. He could be trying to figure out a way to let me down easy, which, honestly, would probably be the best choice. It would save us a lot of exasperation even if the hit to my pride would suck.

I cannot resist saying something more. I hate being quiet.

Amalia: Live a little.

Ezra: 1) Shouldn't it be kissing at
     sundown? Midnight doesn't make
     any sense, PLEASE AMALIA.

Ezra: 2) I'll come over. But just to bring you
     some of this apple-stuffed challah.

Amalia: Oh, is that what the kids are
     calling it these days?

Dad calls me upstairs and that means it's time to light candles and have a seder and stuff myself with the best food on earth. So much for chemistry.

CHAPTER SEVENTEEN

The Law of Electric Charges: Items with like charges repel. Items, however, with opposite charges, well, Those attract.

The most well-known example of this is magnets.

After the candles have burned down and no one can even *think* about eating another bite (with the exception of Ben, who can always think about eating another bite), I go upstairs with Skylar and Ellie, both of whom are staying over. It was perhaps poor planning on my part, given this, to invite Ezra to come make out in my backyard. But I can use my brain; neither of them is coming with us to synagogue tomorrow because school, which means they'll both be out of here pretty early, and I know for a fact that Skylar, at least, needs her beauty sleep.

They'll both be unconscious before Ezra even leaves his house.

Ellie settles in on the floor by my bed and leans up against the mattress. She's in these cute matching penguin pajamas and her dreads are up in a black and white scarf that goes right along with the rest of the outfit. "I'm never eating again," she says.

Skylar kicks her lightly. "Suit yourself. I'm sneaking upstairs in the middle of the night for more honey cakes."

I smirk. "You and your sweet tooth."

She shrugs. "Nothing to be done for it." She scoots over and lays her head on Ellie's shoulder. "I'm gonna miss this."

"Miss what?" says Ellie, eyes already half-shut. Food comas—they are extremely real.

"Just . . . this. How everything is easy."

I raise my eyebrow at her.

"Well, no," she says. "Not everything. I just mean like, you guys. You're accessible. I want to see you, I can see you. I can sit here on my best friend's bedroom floor with my head on my girlfriend's shoulder like it's nothing because we all live just down the street, and the total ridiculousness that is college hasn't hit everyone yet. You know? Where you're like . . . eating ramen nine meals out of ten and studying all the time and like, spending Friday nights crying in the library."

"That's not what college is gonna be like," I say.

Ellie says, "Babe. That's what college is gonna be like."

"For you guys, maybe," I say. "I'm gonna slide through it." I grin and Ellie rolls her eyes and Skylar says, "Oh lord."

I shrug and take a drink of the Cherry Coke I snuck up here and ignore the sudden twist in my stomach that feels like I'm telling a lie. Skylar tilts her head at me and I drink a little more, then stretch. Exaggerated, I know it looks fake.

"I'm about to take a food coma," I say.

"Well," says Skylar, "too bad. We're staying over, which means you have to stay up at least for the beginning of *Atomic Blonde*."

"Oh shit, Charlize Theron. Well, I can probably make that sacrifice."

Ellie says, "Truly kind of you," and we put the movie in and pile around in blankets and pillows like we're little kids at a sleepover.

It's . . . well. It's pretty nice.

It's just after midnight when I catch Ezra's headlights streaming in through my window. At least I *hope* it's Ezra, or there's something extremely clandestine going on around here, and I should be ready to possibly call the cops.

But no; it's him. I recognize his car. It's older, small and efficient. I don't really know shit about cars, but I know it's not one of those cars that you look at and think, *Damn, his parents dropped some CASH on that automobile*. It's one that you think, *That guy takes care of his things.*

It's meticulously maintained. Not a dent or scratch on it, shiny, always. Like he's just taken it through a car wash. Last time I rode in it, it smelled almost new. Just the lightest couple stains from its age, which can't totally be avoided. It's the exact kind of car Ezra Holtz would drive.

Anyway, I recognize it, and it gives me this oddly comfortable feeling of familiarity.

Of course, only now when I have to go outside to meet him as soon as possible do I realize that I made a grave mistake watching *Atomic Blonde* with the girls and totally dozed off so I killed my own plans to look cute. I'm in these ratty pajama shorts that barely cover my ass and an even rattier top—loose and big with a couple holes torn in it. I'm sure my hair is just *inexplicable*.

I sit up as quietly as possible and run my hand through my hair, like that will help. Maybe I can disentangle myself from this jumble of blankets without being noticed. Oh god, I don't know.

I grit my teeth and hold my breath and stand, wrench my ankle free of a twisted sheet, and gently push Ellie's head away from my feet. Then I tiptoe like a cartoon out of my room and down the stairs.

There's not even a prayer of me being able to clean up before I see him, because well, all my clothes are in my room and turning on the light would, in fact, implicate me. So I just purse my lips, blow out a breath, and wrangle my hair in the hair tie I keep around my wrist at all times. And brush my teeth lightning fast. I sneak into the kitchen and snag some Manischewitz and date and honey cake from the fridge, then slide open the back door.

I clench my teeth and hold my breath as it closes, but no motion seems to be coming from inside the house. That's the nice thing about Jewish holidays—well, most of them—as a rule, they involve food and alcohol and the deep, deep sleep one gets just after is basically amazing. It's doubly amazing if it's your parents passed out and you're trying to, you know, meet some boy to make out with in your backyard.

Some boy.
Ezra Effing Holtz.

I walk around the back in bare feet because I somehow forgot shoes, but too late now. When I circle around the side of the house, Ezra is already out of his car, still in his nice dinner clothes (of course), hair managed, shoes on. He looks like he came here on purpose.

Then there's me.

But hey, what else is new?

Ezra raises his eyebrow and whispers, "Catch you in the middle of something?"

"Shut up. Follow me."

He chuckles and closes the distance between us when I turn around, so I can hear every step he takes across the yard just behind mine. *Crunch, crunch, crunch.*

I can feel his height shadowing me—smell his deodorant and the leftover scents of honey and roast chicken and whatever else he had tonight clinging to his clothing fibers. Lord. He smells delicious, and it's a problem.

It's a problem that when he gets so close to me that I can feel him breathe against my hair, I get goose bumps.

Actual. Goose bumps.

I ignore them, or try to, and hope he doesn't notice. How could he, in the dark like this? "We're going into my tree house," I say. "Watch your step on that nail, it'll mess you up."

He follows me up and I watch his head pop through the hole in the ground, watch him pull himself up, the muscles in his forearms flexing as he does. I watch everything, totally fascinated, *embarrassingly* interested in all the little details.

He, thankfully, doesn't say anything.

Maybe he's too busy studying me.

"So this is like, your secret hideout?" he says.

I smile. "Yeah, you could say that."

"This is where you go to think."

"It is."

"And make out with guys on New Year's."

I snort. "Oh, I'm sorry, is that what you think we're doing?"

Ezra's mouth curls up. "I would *never*," he says, putting a hand to his chest, "presume. I'm just curious if that's a regular habit."

I know it's not what he means, I know I should laugh; that's what he wants. But suddenly I see that asshole at the restaurant. I hear him implying that I'm a slut, asking me if I'll redacted his redacted, and Ezra's joke stings.

I blink at the floor. "Uh."

"I'm not . . . I wasn't trying to . . ." He looks up at the ceiling, and I can see the sudden torture on his face now that my eyes are beginning to adjust to the dark. "I'm not saying you have a habit."

That took him a while. Some real effort. To work out how to apologize for something (that, reasonably, wasn't his fault) without letting me know that I have a reputation. Well. Surprise. I already knew.

I say, "I know. Don't worry about it."

"Nah, it was a jerk thing to say. It's not what I meant."

"You?" I say. "Apologizing for being a jerk? It *is* Rosh Hashanah; I forgive you of your debts against me."

He smiles again, just a little. A twitch of his lips. And says, "If I'm being a jerk, I prefer it to be intentional. And not . . . real. So yeah, forgive me."

I relax by degrees, but find myself saying, "You wouldn't be apologizing if you didn't think it was true."

His voice lowers when mine does. "Think what was true?"

"Oh," I say. "You know. My habits."

Ezra scoots closer, and the bag of whatever food he brought crinkles when his leg brushes past it. "Come on."

"No," I say. Suddenly I'm nervous again. I'm feeling guilty and kind of shitty about things that haven't mattered to me in a long time. But look at him. He's so clean and nice and sitting here on the dirty floor of my old treehouse. Meeting up with a girl after dark to make out and who knows what else and not be in love. And I feel like . . . I feel like I'm going to sully him.

Like doing this with me is going to tarnish his reputation or his clothes or his . . . well. Just him. I feel *guilty* looking at him. And slutty. How unfeminist is that? How dare I even be thinking it? I'm embarrassed that it's even a concern, but it's true. He wouldn't be falling all over himself to apologize, to talk around it, if he didn't know my reputation was real.

"You should . . ." I look up over his shoulder, at the moonlight streaming in through the window, illuminating the nothing on the bare floor. The empty walls. We'd always planned to do it up nicer in here but I never followed through. (*jazz hands* Surpriiiise.) "You should know. Getting into anything with me. It's okay if it was just a one-time thing."

"Amalia."

"You just need to be aware, okay? People find out about anything, your reputation is probably gonna be shot." I shrug, like it doesn't matter. "People—people have strong opinions about me. They know me for ditching class and smoking weed and just being out-of-control, you know. You know exactly what they think. And they think I'm a slut."

"Please," he says. "Like that means anything."

"Well. It kind of does. It means something for me. And you should know that every rumor I've ever heard about myself is at least half true. I know it's almost never that way, but in my case, turns out it is. So no, I don't have a habit of bringing people up here to make out, but I do have some *habits* I guess, and you're this sterling valedictorian, and maybe you should consider that before you decide you want to get involved."

Ezra blows out a breath. "Amalia."

"What?"

"You think I care about any of that?"

"I—yeah, Ezra. I think you probably do. Don't tell me it hasn't crossed your mind."

His lips thin, but then he thinks for a second and says, "Okay. Yes. It's crossed my mind. But I just . . . I just don't think that matters right now? I know what I'm doing. You know what you're doing."

A smile touches my mouth. "And what is that?"

"Wishing each other happy new year."

I laugh and Ezra's mouth ticks up.

"What'd you bring me?" I say.

"Apples and honey."

"Oh, how daring and original. Apples and honey on Rosh Hashanah."

He narrows his eyes and says, "Be nice to me or I'll take them home. And this honey is the real deal; Tate got it from the farmers' market with the comb inside."

"Oh, the *farmers' market*."

"Don't act like you don't want it."

I do. Of course I do. When he takes it out of the paper bag, I can see the rich color of the honey even in the dark. It's amber, almost brown, not pale yellow like grocery store honey is. It's going to taste like the hive it came from, like *depth*. My mouth is actually watering.

"Just give me the food and no one gets hurt, Holtz."

He says, "Say *please*."

"If you don't hand it over, I'm not giving you this date and honey cake."

"Funny way you have of pronouncing *please*."

I smile with my teeth.

He pushes the honey and apples toward me and I say, "Or the Manischewitz."

"Oh no."

"Oh yes."

Ezra says, "I'll take the cake. Keep your adult syrup."

"Please. If I had to drink this tonight, so do you."

Ezra laughs. "I'm okay with sneaking out if necessary. Breaking the law is not for me."

I roll my eyes and swirl the wine around in the bottle. "Please. As if you haven't been drinking since you were thirteen."

He takes a bite of the honey cake and mutters, "Oh, wow, this is good." Then says, "It's different. I've been drinking with parents. Or like, at official holiday dinners. I don't think the cops will buy *We were celebrating Rosh Hashanah, officers,* in the middle of the night in your treehouse. While all the adults are asleep."

"Ugh," I say. "Who's going to call the cops?"

"I will, you delinquent."

I shove him in the shoulder and set the wine bottle back down on the wood floor.

Ezra says, "I don't know if you've thought through the possible consequences of our hooking up to *your* reputation." He pushes his glasses up on his nose and I actually clench my fingers on my thigh. My stomach kind of tightens? Jesus, it's so endearing. Ezra is doing things that are *endearing* and if he could just *stop*. If he could just not look at me like that, like he's studying me. Like he's challenging me, because he's always, always challenging me.

He's wry, almost, eyebrow cocked, waiting for me to respond.

I crunch into an apple and savor the floral, woody honey on my tongue for one silent second before I say, "I'm gonna need you to explain that."

"Look at you," he says. "You just don't give a shit, do you?"

I swallow. I'm—I'm glad he sees it that way. I'm glad everyone else seems to. That's what I've cultivated for years, right? I want to say, "Nope! Sure don't!" But instead I focus on the taste in my mouth. I focus on the apple and the honey and the smell of fall in the air, and I don't look directly at Ezra's face.

He says, "Word gets out that you're hooking up with me, it's gonna destroy the whole devil-may-care thing you've got going, you know. *That kid? The valedictorian? The one who doesn't smile? Doesn't he study calculus to have fun?*"

I laugh out loud. "Do you study calculus for fun?"

"Of course I don't." He cocks his head. "Trigonometry or bust."

I groan but I'm laughing.

"*Amalia Yaabez is not who we thought. His hands are way too methodical for her.*"

"Methodical?" I say. "I'm sorry, how much time do you think people spend talking about your hands?"

"I bet you talk about my hands."

I choke and he takes another bite of the honey cake, shifts forward so his knee is touching mine.

"I try not to discuss you or your body parts with anyone."

"Mm," he says. "See? That reputation. You've got one to maintain."

"No, I'm just busy talking about other things that interest me."

"Oh really," he says flatly. "Like what?"

"Like . . . calculus."

Ezra laughs. Loud, a little too loud for comfort in the dead of night, but I like it. I'm enjoying it; I'm enjoying *all* of this.

I busy myself with the apples and honey and don't reach for the alcohol. It's less fun to drink by yourself. "Like chemistry, actually."

"Yeah?" he says.

"Yeah. I'm . . . kind of into it."

"You sound like you're admitting to being into clown porn or something."

I about spit out my apple. "Excuse me?"

He shrugs. "You're just . . . weirdly embarrassed. To be into chemistry. I'm judging you hard. Clearly. *Oh no, Amalia is a nerd.*"

"I'm not a nerd."

He says, "Eh."

I glare at him.

158

"I'm not the one going on about chemistry during a secret rendezvous."

"Please. You're *always* more likely to be the one going on about chemistry, in or out of a secret rendezvous."

"My point stands. Plus, I don't like chemistry."

I snort. "Bet you aced it."

"Well," he says, "I'm good at a lot of things I hate."

I say, "That's cocky."

"It's not cocky. It's true. Are you thinking about going into it? For a living?"

I shrug. "Maybe." It's so dark, and my eyes may have adjusted but we're still not a whole lot more than silhouettes, apart from where the moonlight hits. It feels safe for some reason, feels like we're the only two people in the world. Feels like what I say here stays in the treehouse. And maybe that's why I say, "I don't know, Ezra, it's hard. To have wanted something for so long, to have built this whole life, this whole . . . identity around it. And to have it taken from me."

He's quiet for a minute. "Is it taken? Really?"

"Well," I say, "it's just not the way I'd always dreamed about it."

"That can't be easy."

"No."

"I mean, I know who you hang around with. I see you at school. Ellie, Skylar. Everyone knows they're off to arts schools and stuff."

"Christ, rub it in," I say.

"Not trying to. Just saying that has to feel shitty."

I want to be offended. Want to wrinkle my nose and tell him to fuck off with his deep character observations.

But I'm not and I don't. All I can say is, "Yeah." And then, "I haven't even told her."

"Well. It's not like you owe anyone anything about yourself."

"I guess . . . I guess that's true. She's my best friend, though; it feels like I do."

"Isn't she your ex, too?"

"Yeah." I laugh. "Whaddya gonna do?"

"Damn, do you have *any* straight friends? Besides me?"

I do a quick mental inventory—I hang out with Skylar more than anyone, and with Ellie, and the kids at smoker's corner. A few fringe friends in art. Sasha and Brent and Asia and the rest of the kids from the Cool Partier crowd. I say, "Well. Queers of a feather."

He laughs again, all loud and clear and genuine. I want to stretch out in it, luxuriate in the sound.

"You wouldn't be the first person to have not gotten things exactly as they wanted them, Amalia. Is all I'm saying."

"Oh? And what is it that you want that you can't have?"

He looks at me, and for a second he's totally raw. His eyes are open and unguarded by the typical mask of arrogance he wears. He just . . . looks at me. And I'm afraid of what he might say. It's such an odd reaction. But I am.

He blinks away then says, "I don't know, Amalia. Lots of things. Freedom, I guess. I want to go into engineering. Possibly in alternative energy. I have plans. But I've always had them, and there's no deviation. I've never had time to play soccer like I used to want to or go to a bunch of parties—"

"I've seen you at parties."

"Yeah. Like two."

I shrug. "Still."

"I have friends, but not the way you do."

"What about Mike?" I say. "He's still your friend. And those academic guys—Isaac and Marcus? Who else . . . Iris."

"One," he says, "how do you know my entire circle of friends?"

I blush and he looks very pleased with himself.

"Two, it's different. I don't have people from every social group, everywhere, who love me. And that kind of simple, easy, *I do what I want*, cutting class to smoke weed thing. I don't have that."

"Do you want it, though?" I say. "Do you really want that?"

"Sometimes."

My eyes are sparkling; I can feel it. Can feel the smile in my cheeks. "Do you want to cut class and smoke weed with me, Ezra?"

He shifts closer to me. "Nah."

"Look at me, calling your bluff." I lean in.

His hands are in my hair. "You calling me a liar?"

I'm nervous, I don't know why I'm nervous. "Mmhmm."

"I'm not a liar. I'm just distracted."

"There you go again, with that word."

"Well." He kisses me. "You're distracting."

He kisses me again. We don't come up for air until the nighttime turns gray.

CHAPTER EIGHTEEN

TEST GROUP
LINA AND JANELLE

 INT: *Bedroom. Wall is baby blue with purple striping. Twinkle lights are strung from corner to corner across the ceiling. Unclear whose room.*

VIEW: *Lina, hair in a ponytail with little braids woven through it, comes smiling into the frame.*

Lina: *So I guess it's my turn to give an update on the project?*

Lina twirls her hair, one finger caught in a little braid that's fallen out of her ponytail. It's complicated, several thin little braids weaving around her head, but not haphazard.

Lina: *It's going well. We, uh. Went out on that date and it turns out we do have quite a bit in common. We made it through the first two sets of questions, too. The silly, fun ones like your favorite food-related memory—*

Janelle glides into the frame, eyebrows raised. She's wearing bright orange lipstick and her lips are quirked up. Lina jumps.

Janelle: *Your mom let me in.*

Lina: *Holy shit.*

Janelle: *Can you say that on a school assignment?*

Lina (looking quickly at camera): *Well I guess I've said it already and I'm not starting over.*

Janelle: *That's what you get for starting without me.*

Janelle gets up out of her wheelchair and walks a couple feet to Lina's bed, sits on it. Looks directly in the frame

Janelle: *So what has Lina said? Have you been answering everything already? Everything we were supposed to cover?*

Lina: *No, I'd just gotten started.*

Janelle: *Come sit with me.*

Lina (smiling in a slow small way that looks unintentional): *What the lady wants.*

VIEW: *The camera shifts so we see Lina's jeans for a while, hear rustling in the background and Janelle giggling. Lina pulls the camera back up, angled down at both of them from what may or may not be a selfie stick.*

Janelle: *So.*

She scoots close to Lina so they're shoulder to shoulder. Lina scrapes her teeth over her lip, cheeks a little flushed. Janelle, for her part, is looking a tad smug about all of it.

Janelle: *We've made it through two stages of your questions. What fictional character we'd invite out for a night and what we'd do.*

Lina: *What we would do if we won the lottery.*

Janelle: *Worst fear.*

Lina (laying her head on Janelle's shoulder, casual, like it's a nothing gesture already): *We haven't hit tier three yet. Maybe we should . . . I don't know, should we do that tonight?*

Lina looks over at Janelle, who suddenly has a furrow on her brow. Nails clicking.

Janelle: *Have you read the stuff that's on there?*

Lina, shrugging: *Yeah.*

Janelle, eyeing the camera: *I don't . . . maybe we don't ruin this just yet?*

Lina, frowning: *Just yet?*

Janelle: *Okay, well hey, turn off the camera.*

End recording.

It's Friday night and I'm here. Working.

I haven't seen the light of day in ages, it feels like. Well. The dark of night, I guess. Everything, everything has turned into work. It's either working on the project with Ezra (or . . . well, in the interest of representing the situation fairly, "working on the project" *waggle eyebrows waggle eyebrows hint hint* with Ezra) or studying for my other classes so I can get into school and get who even knows what kind of career, and I'm not going to lie.

I've been okay about it.

Tonight, I'm pissed off.

I'm sitting on my bedroom floor alone with a Coke and an AP English syllabus, working out the exact possible meaning of the symbolism in *Old Man and the Sea*. It's an absolute riot. Who doesn't just fall all over themselves with love for Ernest Hemingway?

Skylar texts me:

Skylar: Come out.

I take a few minutes before I even respond

Amalia: been there done that lol

She texts me again:

Skylar: UGH TONIGHT YOU DORK

I tell her I can't, I'm studying, and just totally ignore the eighteen bazillion question marks she shoots back at me. In fairness, if I were anyone but my actual self, I wouldn't believe me either.

My stoner group chat goes off, too, and someone eventually says they're about to cut me out of it.

Fine. I don't care.

I kind of care.

I don't care about the old man or the sea.

I rub my temples and stare at the book, this wretched, evil book, and think of all the things I could be doing that are not this.

I could be out with Skylar.

I could be at temple, hanging out with whoever shows up tonight.

I could be doing a night hike and getting drunk somewhere in the woods.

I could be researching places to go this weekend, do something cool none of my friends has done. Cliff diving or something. Oh *man*, I could be cliff diving.

I'm staring off wistfully like the ingénue in a musical, imagining jumping off a rock into the cold depths below, and it's amazing.

Just thinking about it is amazing.

But no.

What I am doing is this. I have ONE LIFE and I am spending it on my BEDROOM FLOOR reading about an old guy and a big fish.

GOD.

I must make a noise of exasperation out loud because Ben peeks his head into my room and says, "Nerd. What are you doing?"

I slam my head down into my book and grumble, "Nothing."

"You studying?"

"Ugh. Yes. Please come kill me. Just go get one of Kaylee's dork-ass swords and stab me in the back while I'm not looking. I don't want to see it coming."

Ben says, "Thank god, I thought you'd never ask."

I flip him the bird and he laughs.

"Seriously, dude, what are you doing up here in the dark?"

"Studying."

"Why?"

I sigh and turn around. "Because, *Ben,* someone told me I needed to if I was gonna fix my shit. *Someone* told me I was smart."

He scratches the back of his head and looks up at the corner of my room. "Couldn't have been me."

"Nah. Of course not."

"Well," he says after a minute, "if you're gonna be gracing us all with your presence tonight, come downstairs. I'll grill you on Mark Twain and whatever while you help us cook."

"Hemingway."

He rolls his eyes. "Worse. Seriously, come on."

I stare down at my book.

At my phone.

At the freedom I am voluntarily saying no to. I feel . . . overwhelmed. Even with Ben doing this suddenly super cool helpful older brother thing, even though it's not like Hemingway is particularly hard. It's just so much to tackle.

I'm so annoyed with myself that all I want to do is leave.

Annoyed that in the three hours I've been down here going over chemistry and psychology and trig and literature, I've spent an hour and a half on Twitter. And like . . . Instagram. It's not even because it's interesting! I started seeing all the same posts over and over!

I just don't know how to lock my brain into work mode, from *KILL ME PLEASE* mode.

L-a-z-y.

"Amalia. I am starving."

I blink back at him.

"Good lord, Ben. Fine. You've probably eaten nineteen meals today."

He shrugs, grins, and pulls me up by the hand.

I head down the stairs, book under my arm, and pass Kaylee who's on the couch, feet kicked up. She's reading *Anna Karenina*, I shit you not, and she looks actually into it.

Anna. Karenina.

"Kaylee, you've got to be kidding me."

"I love Tolstoy's use of language." She eyes me over the top of the book and goes back to it. I groan. I am surrounded by these people at all turns; maybe she and Ezra *should* have hooked up.

Mom and Dad are both already in the kitchen. Dad's doing something with a whole chicken and mom is at the island that, truthfully, this kitchen is *not* big enough to justify. She mixing something that involves pomegranate and pepper and cayenne; I smell the sweet bite in the air when I pass her. Man, it smells divine.

"Finally," Dad says. "Amalia. You, my dear, are on onion duty."

"Noooooo," I say.

"As though studying in that loft all night wasn't already making you cry. We're just shifting the cause, not the effect."

"Traitorous," I say, glaring at Ben. I hate cutting onions. We all do. Every single person in my family except Kaylee has a wicked sensitivity to them; one time Dad was upstairs cutting into one, and I literally started crying from all the way upstairs in my room.

I'm mad at Kaylee for loving reading when I snag a pair of goggles and a couple onions. I assume Dad will be shoving these, sliced, into the chicken's butt. I start cutting and sniffling.

Ben is loving every minute of it. He kicks back at the kitchen table and pulls up something on his phone, then says, "Alright. Molls. What is the central theme of *The Old Man and the Sea?*"

I say, "Kaylee. Get me your sword."

She yells, "WHAT?" from the living room, and Mom shoots me a look.

Ben snaps at me. "Central theme, Molls, we're wasting daylight."

"This is stupid."

"It's not stupid," he says.

Dad says, eyes still on the chicken, "It's about a man fighting nature. The conflict with the marlin. Hemingway was such a *manly man* it's all in his work. It's about strength and mastery."

Mom says, "It's been forever since I've read that but I always thought it had more to do with him and himself than it did the fish. The fish is a stand-in for some real issues he had. What kind of person goes to those lengths for a fish?"

"I don't know, it—"

"NERDS," I say. "You are literally everywhere. Between this entire family and Ezra Holtz, I'm about to lose it."

Dad turns to face me, hands coated in grease and spices, and says, "You and Ezra have been getting close."

"Nope. Nope nope, that's not something I'm talking about."

Ben waggles his eyebrows. "I don't know whether to make fun of you or go hurl. Dude, of all the guys."

"Nothing," I say. "Nothing is going on with Ezra Holtz, I only brought him up because everyone in here refuses to shut up about this stuff and cook and you guys are all the same."

"I resent that," says Ben.

I whirl on him, brandishing the knife. "Who's the guy asking about central literary themes while we're trying to cook, huh?"

Ben laughs and the kitchen goes a little quiet while we work. My eyes are burning, even with the goggles. There's really nothing I can do to protect myself; it's why we all switch off when Kaylee's being an ass. Onions are a nightmare.

Mom sidles up next to me and says, adding her pomegranate mixture to a saucepan and reducing it on the stove, "For what it's worth, I don't see the issue with you liking Ezra."

"I don't like Ezra." And it's true. I *don't*. I like fooling around with Ezra and those are two very different things.

"Well," she says. "Even so."

"He's arrogant. He's a know-it-all. He's . . . I don't know. He talks about school like it matters." *He climbs mountains for fun. He's got a smile that makes you go weak in the knees. He's funny, shockingly wry. NO. N-O.*

Mom says, "That's bad? Caring about school?"

"It's not for me."

Mom purses her lips as the sauce starts to steam and concentrate.

"What?" I say.

She shrugs. Looks out through the pass-through at Kaylee reading *Anna Karenina*. At Dad focusing so hard on getting that chicken absolutely perfectly prepared. At Ben, waiting to quiz me again at the table, scrolling through his phone, forehead scrunched in concentration. "I just want to say that it doesn't make a person weird or useless. Or *uncool*." She says it with extremely uncool parental air quotes.

"What doesn't?"

"Choosing to care about things."

And that—that makes me go quiet.

I care about things. The wrong things, apparently, according to every art school on the east coast, but, I do.

I don't . . . I don't look down on people for caring about stuff.

. . . do I?

"MOLLS."

"What?" I blink. I'm done with the onion, thank the lord, my eyes are streaming. I take off the goggles and rub my hands over my eyes, hard. "Sorry, what?" It's clear Ben's been saying my name for a minute.

"How does Hemingway's simple use of language complement the text and its themes?"

I take a second, intending to shoot back something smartass, something that makes it clear that none of this matters to me.

Then I glance back at Mom, who is pouring the sauce over the chicken. She's a little too still.

Listening.

I sigh. And I actually think.

"I guess it complements the narrator's voice. Which kind of reflects Hemingway's views both on masculinity and how men think."

Ben doesn't make fun of me.

He's looking down at his phone, but he's smiling.

CHAPTER NINETEEN

TEST GROUP
ARIEL AND CARLOS

 SUBJ. LINE: STUDY

SENDER: Ariel Cade

CONTENT OF E-MAIL: I have spent the last six days studiously plodding through this list of questions with Carlos, and let me tell you what I have learned: that a person should not entrust random strangers with plotting out their love life.

I'm not trying to be a jerk here, okay? And Carlos isn't The Worst as much as he is exhausting. To me. He's dated a bunch of girls before, girls I like, some of them at least, so he can't be just generally bad; maybe this isn't your fault. But I'm telling you that SOMETIMES getting to know someone better makes it worse. SOMETIMES you actually kind of like someone from a distance, and then you find out that underneath that hardcore punk exterior lies a hardcore punk interior and they find out that the reason you wear puff sleeves and necklines buttoned up to your throat and baby pink lip gloss is because you LIKE those things, dammit. And both of you find yourselves wanting to die.

We haven't gotten to your last, epically vulnerable set of questions yet, but at this point I am concerned that his worst memory will be that time his mom threw his Dead Kennedys album in the fireplace and I am absolutely POSITIVE he is going to sleep through the personality trait I am most embarrassed about (if you must know, it's my need to correct everyone's grammar; I know it's terrible and obnoxious but it kills me to refrain). We practically sleep through meetings now anyway.

I don't know how we're going to survive four entire minutes of eye contact.

I'm not even THINKING about kissing him so do not even BEGIN to suggest it.

—Ariel

P.S. Absolutely do not let this get back to Carlos or I will ruin your lives.

⚗

It has been a while since I could pick up a brush.

Since I could run my fingers over a canvas without feeling sick to my stomach.

My chemistry textbook sits open behind me, pages highlighted and dog-eared, notes scribbled in the margins in handwriting, that, even to myself, even though it's my *own* freaking handwriting, is a little tricky to decipher.

I write that way when I'm interested in something. As it turns out, the idea that hydrogen peroxide will actually change forms and shift into water if left out in a clear container for long enough, is fascinating.

The idea that just leaving something as seemingly defined, scientific, as a chemical out in the open, in a new environment, will literally change its composition. Wow. What the hell. It doesn't seem possible, and I am such an utter dork for being capable of getting excited about that, but here I am and there's nothing to be done for it.

I, Amalia Yaabez, like *science*.

Put that on your Bunsen burner and smoke it.

So there's that, there's the bizarre thing happening in my brain.

And if I can do that, if I can learn to enjoy something as boring (I thought) as freaking chemistry, maybe I can paint.

Maybe I can do something I love, without furiously ripping the canvas to shreds like painting took itself away from me.

I pick up a brush.

My hands are shaking.

Everything is set up exactly the way it should be—paints and brushes and canvas, the perfect light streaming through the window so the canvas already looks magical. Already looks like it should be lighting up the singular bright piece in an otherwise dark Rembrandt. Is it starting that's difficult?

Is that usually where I come up short?

No, it's not. Today is different.

Typically starting is easy; it's pushing through to the end that paralyzes me. That makes me want to toss the half-done seascape or whatever and start something new, something full of blank, perfect potential. But now I'm sitting here and I can't even get pigment on the page.

I can't start. I feel like everything I do is going to mess it up, and how ridiculous is that? It's not like anyone's even going to see it. It's not like *this* is for a grade, not like anything I create is going into a portfolio. This is just for me. And even still, it's too hard.

I don't have to paint. I could pop out some charcoals. Some pastels. I could draw.

That's not what I want to do.

I want to *paint*. I *love*. To paint.

A frustrated noise escapes my throat and I glance up at the clock; Ezra is going to be here in like a half hour and I can't even get *started*. I swear, last year I could knock out a whole piece in a half hour if I was going for speed.

It wouldn't be detailed, perfect, beautiful. But it would be *good*. Good enough to look at and say, "Hell yeah, self. You did this in thirty minutes? Post this shit on Instagram and brag about it."

Now . . . nothing.

I'm not inspired.

Which I hate, *I hate*.

I used to say that people who needed inspiration to work were amateurs and I still believe that, kind of, it's just that now I think I am one of them.

God, what a nightmare.

I don't even know how much time passes, me just staring at nothing.

Into the canvassular abyss that is probably some incredible metaphor for my whole entire life.

What I do know is that if I can count on Ezra for anything, it is to be on time. And by "on time," I mean at least two minutes early.

He rings the doorbell, and I don't even move to answer it. I'm busy sitting here.

Kaylee gets it, and she is welcome.

I hear Ezra coming up the stairs, and I think, *You look pathetic, Amalia, honestly. Stop. Get up. Paint something, anything, so he doesn't walk in here and see that you are completely worthless*, but what I do not do is: that.

Ezra walks into my room.

He nearly closes the door behind him, leaves it open just a crack so my parents won't kill him if they venture up here, and I am sitting here like a lump on the chair.

"Busy?" he says.

And I burst into tears.

"Shit," he says.

God, I'm so embarrassed. What is wrong with me?

I don't even look at him because that can only possibly make it worse; I don't want to see him looking pitying or terrified at a girl crying or any number of things I am positive he looks like right now. I want to pretend this isn't happening. I want to uninvite him over, this boy who I allegedly want to want to put his tongue in my mouth and who now is watching me be the most unkissable, un-everything-able version of myself.

Either that, or I want to go back in time and stop myself from sitting down at the one thing that reminds me how much of a failure I am, that I can't seem to *stop* failing at in a million different ways.

I cover my face with my hands, wipe away these super attractive tears, which probably destroys my eyeliner, and look at the blank nothing that I quit at literally before I even *started* it, and just lose it again.

Might as well go all in. If you can't accept me at my ILLOGICAL PATHETIC WEEPINGEST, you don't deserve me at my nakedest.

I feel Ezra's long, slender fingers on my shoulder, but he doesn't say anything else. He just stands there, applying gentle pressure to my skin. I could shrug him off. But I don't want to. I'm a little quieter. He runs his thumb over my back, a place he is familiar with. Not that it's anywhere sexy—it's the curve of my shoulder. Still, he's touched it enough times and having him touch me there again is grounding, comforting.

I stutter in a breath, feeling less out of control and more just . . . stupid. And I wrestle my face into submission. Okay. Okay, I am fine.

I breathe out. Slowly. Like I'm at the doctor's office—breath, two, three.

Then I spin slowly around. I say brightly, "Hey!"

Ezra raises an eyebrow and says, "Hey, Taylor Momsen."

I groan. "Yeah, I'm sure my eyeliner is a freaking mess."

"Eh. Matches the rest of everything in here."

I shove him and he stumbles back, smirking. It's irritating, in one way—the little jab. In another way, it's familiar. It's the way we talk to each other and I like it. It doesn't feel like he's actually insulting me, it feels more like . . . more like he's saying, *I know you.*

I say, "You asshole."

He shrugs. "You okay?"

I say, "Yeah, what, do I not look okay?"

"No, obviously, you're right. Frequently, when I'm feeling average, I find myself crying in my room in front of an easel."

"Good, glad to know I'm not alone then."

Ezra runs his hand through his hair and lets it rest on the back of his neck. "Seriously though, are you okay?"

"I—no. No, I guess I'm not."

"Hit me with it."

"We're supposed to be working."

"We are working," Ezra says. He pulls a familiar slip of paper from his backpack and scans the list of questions we forced on our study participants. "What was the last thing that made you cry?"

I roll my eyes. "We're not supposed to answer those; the test subjects are."

"Humor me."

I rub my hands under my eyes, get my emotions a little more under control. "Better?" I say.

"You're golden." He smiles—genuinely smiles, and I am caught off-guard.

I can feel it in my chest, like a spring loosening.

I say, "Well. Good." Then: "Tell me I'm not a failure."

"Amalia," he says. "You are not a failure."

"Liar."

"Unfair."

"I feel like . . ." I don't even know how to say this, it's so vulnerable. It's so . . . like . . . it's like vivisecting myself. It's the kind of thing I wouldn't even say to a friend. But then again, Ezra isn't a friend, is he? He's just some guy I've known a while. Some boy I'm fooling around with. And maybe that is why I say: "I feel like there's nothing in my life I've really succeeded at. I wanted to be an artist, and I couldn't. I want to be an academic now and like, I'm doing okay, but I have to kill myself every night to make it happen. I'm kind of a shitty friend, being jealous of Skylar all the time and totally ditching out on the smoker's corner kids. I'm not great at relationships either, like, romantic ones."

"I don't know about that," he says.

"What we have isn't exactly romantic, Holtz."

"Well," he says, "touché."

"I'm like . . . I think I'm That Friend everyone has."

Ezra scoots a sweatshirt aside with his foot and sinks down onto my carpet. He criss-crosses his legs and leans back on his hands. "Elaborate."

"That friend. Who's kind of wild and crazy and reckless. The one you invite to the party because you know she's going to make it a great time for everyone. She's probably going to make out with someone of who knows what gender while you're there and then she'll have some *amazing* stories to tell after and god, she's so fun. That's just Amalia, my wild, unpredictable best friend. Twirling her way through life making everyone else's interesting. The *Artiste*. I'm a fucking manic pixie dream girl, Ezra."

A frown flickers across his face. "You think it's a character flaw that you're *interesting*?"

"I'm not interesting. Not really. I'm a collection of things people think are fun and fascinating from a distance. As a whole person, though? I've built this entire life. This *person*. And what does it even matter? I'm not the kind of person who has meaningful relationships and makes differences in people's lives and gets what I want, am I? I'm the kind of person who makes plans and when they shatter, I shatter with them and no one cares because I'm fine, I'll be fine. I'll just go skydive or something or have a torrid affair with an older French boy while I'm cavorting through Tuscany—"

"Tuscany is in Italy."

"Oh, shut *up*."

"I can't."

"Well that's the freaking truth."

Ezra rolls his eyes. "No. I can't just sit here and listen to you saying all this shit about yourself, Amalia."

I blink back new frustrated tears, and then I'm frustrated about *those*. "It's true. You know it's true."

"That what? You're too wild to live your own life? You're just too much of a free spirit to be a full human?"

I shrug. It feels kind of weird and self-important now that I'm hearing it coming from his mouth.

"I think it's how people think of me," I say. "I think—you know, since I started staying in to *study*"—I pause to fake gag and Ezra rolls his eyes—"most of my friends have stopped texting me. I've seen them a little. Here and there, I guess. But it's not like . . . it's not like I'm hanging out every time they are. Not like they text me all the time."

"Have you texted them?"

I pick at the carpet. "Not a lot. I guess. No I get it, communication is a two-way thing. It's just weird when it becomes clear that a whole lot of people you hang out with are going to forget you exist. It's fine. I'm fine." I set my jaw and say, "Let's work, yeah? I'm sure we have data to chart."

Ezra furrows his brow, then says, almost like a question, "No."

"No?"

He says, more resolutely this time, "No. No, we're ahead of schedule right now and what you need is to get out of this house."

I almost laugh out loud. "Who are you? Seriously, get out your notebook."

He grabs my hand. "Nah." Pulls me up. "It's Everett Andrews's birthday and I am *certain* he's someone you used to hang around with."

"Yeah, I guess. I mean, I still do kind of hang around with him."

"So you'd probably be able to take him up on the half-way open invitation to his house party tonight."

"Yeah. If I had time."

"It's Saturday night. You have time."

I blink up at him. "What is going on? You beg me to stay on task and now I am and you're trying to get me to ditch studying and go party?"

Ezra shrugs with just one shoulder, that never-smiling mouth tugging up. "You've got me curious. I'm intrigued at whatever manic pixie life it is you're dangling out there. Come on." He bites his lip, looking downright mischievous. It's too much. "Show me how the other half lives."

CHAPTER TWENTY

TEST GROUP
SAM AND RILEY

Riley: JESUS.

Sam: Well, my friends call me Sam

Riley: Stop. You are exhausting.

Sam: Nah, you like me.

Riley: Only because we haven't gotten to phase three yet.

Sam: Look at that not-denial

Sam: You liiiiiiiiiike me

Sam: You like LIKE like me

Sam: Riley

Sam: hello

Riley: W H A T

Sam: u like me

Sam: is all im trying to say

Riley: I mean I thought I made that clear. What with all the making out we did last night?

Sam: I just wanted to be SURE

Sam: so cool now that that's settled

Riley: Give me your deepest, darkest secret

Sam: I don't think that's on the list, Ri.

Riley: Don't be a chicken shit

Sam: I liked the prequel trilogy

Riley: . . .

Riley: I'm assuming you don't mean of STAR WARS

Riley: I'm ASSUMING you mean SOME OTHER less famous prequel trilogy that is not complete sacrilege because there is no way you can mean that you ENJOYED ~i DoN't LiKe SaNd~

Sam: IT'S COARSE

Sam: IT'S ROUGH

Riley: oh my god

Sam: IT'S IRRITATING

Sam: Is he wrong

Sam: Does it not get everywhere

Riley: That's it. I want an experiment divorce

Sam: you can't do that

Riley: No. These differences are irreconcilable

Sam: would you say they're irritating

Riley: Yes

Sam: so

Sam: like sand

When I hop in Ezra's car, he's blasting klezmer (eastern European Jewish music). Golem is about to rip a hole through those speakers, it's so loud.

"You wanna turn that down?" I say. Shout.

Ezra yells back, "Absolutely not."

I frown at him, exaggeratedly.

"Come on, Amalia, where's your holiday spirit?"

"What?"

"Don't tell me you're one of those *Rosh Hashanah music and décor just get put out earlier and earlier every year, ugh, turn down the holiday music PLEASE* kind of people."

He kicks the car into gear and we drive off.

"Ezra. I have no idea what you're talking about."

"As if you haven't heard the Jewish music blasting through *every* mall and department store for the last month."

I actually start laughing. Now I know exactly what he's doing. "I mean really, if I have to hear Matisyahu in the craft store ONE MORE TIME."

Ezra cackles. Straight up cackles.

He does not turn his "holiday music" down.

He smiles right at me, mischievous and free and loose and something tells me he set up his radio, this whole gag, just for me.

I don't know why something as small as someone's musical life being momentarily switched up because I exist in it puts butterflies in my stomach.

But lord help me. It does.

🧪

Everett Andrews's house is not huge. It's not like those giant block party houses in every eighties and nineties teen movie where kids are like . . . wrecking crystal vases and hanging out in the indoor pool and weaving in and out of the eight-thousand-square-foot marble kitchen splashing beer on the travertine.

It's a little bigger than mine, by a bathroom and a couple bedrooms. Nice. Everett has money.

But most of it is in the *yard*.

No one is congregated inside the house because everyone is spilling all that cheap beer outside. He's got like, five wooded acres and his parents completely tricked it out. There's little winding faerie paths through the woods and an amazing fire pit and a hot tub, and I would *live* out here if it were an option.

I kind of used to, I guess. Before this semester, this last month, month or two, when I have been forced to reconfigure all my life plans and learn how to be an introvert.

I walk beside Ezra into the backyard and Everett sees me almost immediately. "Oh daaaaaaaamn!" His smile is wide and genuinely happy; it's always been infectious. He plays baseball, and most of the baseball guys are pretty popular so that's his crowd. One of the crowds I've moved effortlessly through when I've chosen to.

I smile back. It's also genuine; I forgot how much I liked Everett. It rushes back immediately. "Oh heeeyyyyy!" I yell across the yard.

"The party is HERE," he says. "I didn't know you were coming, Yaabez."

"Ah," I say, faking offense. "I guess I'll just have to head out if I'm not invited." I say it with a glint in my eye, and for a second, I forget about academia, I forget about work, I forget all the complications with Ezra and my pity party and I just . . . remember who I've been. The life I've had before all my plans went down the drain.

Everett says, "Oh no you don't," and grabs me by the wrist, spinning me into his arms. There's something Top 40 streaming through the in-ground speakers his parents must have blown a truly RIDICULOUS amount of money on. I throw my arms around his neck and move against him, and he slides his hands down my back, eyes sparkling.

"Where you been?" he says.

"Everywhere."

I hear it as I say it. The manic pixie thing. The whirling, twirling, phantom mystery girl persona that I fall so easily into now, and it makes me mad. But it's not like I try to do this. Is it a problem, I wonder, if this is the person I am?

Everett rolls his eyes, but he's still smiling. "Yeah that sounds right."

He pulls me a little closer, dances with me just a *little* dirty. I play right along with it. Everett and I have never been anything more than friends, never even fooled around. Unless you count the one time everyone got a little high and decided for some reason that playing spin-the-bottle was a good idea, and Everett and I wound up making out and both being kind of embarrassed about it. He's hot; there is *zero* denying that. That—like I said—totally infectious smile, dark brown eyes, darker brown skin, broad shoulders, long legs. He's hot. And funny; Everett is one of those jocks who has the innate ability to make everyone feel comfortable in fifteen seconds flat. Mostly because he knows how to make people laugh. He's going to school on a baseball scholarship to be a therapist, and wow is that the correct career choice for him. But anyway, nothing's ever gone down between us. We're friends, we've always been friends, and our hips might be moving a little filthily right now but that's just what you do when Ariana Grande comes on. Freaking 'God is a Woman.' Who isn't powerless against it?

"Who'd you bring?" he says, tipping his chin up at Ezra, who is trying his level best not to be uncomfortable, but alone in a big crowd like this where he probably knows next to no one, he's looking just a *little* uncomfortable.

Running his hand back through his hair, adjusting his glasses. I pull back from Everett and walk the few steps back to Ezra. His shoulders immediately fall from where they were—basically by his ears.

"Ezra Holtz?" I say.

"Oh shit, right! I know you."

"You do?" Ezra's eyebrow jumps up.

"Yeah, man. We're in speech together, that's where I recognize you from. Talking Nazi-punching and stuff in a real red classroom. I remember that." He says, "Plus you're what, valedictorian or something?"

"Going for it," Ezra says. He's not exactly smiling but he's pleased, I can tell. He's doing that little non-grin with his mouth, this tapping thing with his fingers on his chest. He's enjoying the recognition from someone like Everett. Everyone does. I am absolutely gonna give him shit about it later, though.

"You don't remember me. It's cool; I have a thing for faces."

Ezra actually laughs. "Of course I know you. Baseball god. Everyone knows you."

Everett throws his head back and laughs and says, "Don't bullshit me. Go get a drink. Enjoy the party." He looks at me and says, "You, find me later? Or hit me up after the party some time. We need to catch up. It's been too long."

"You're right. No, it definitely has."

Everett heads off to play host and I smile at Ezra. "Star struck?"

"No."

"You should have seen the look on your face." I press my hand to my chest dramatically. "Oh, oh Everett? Of *course* I know who you are. Please. Sign my pecs."

"You are an absolute menace," he says.

I say back, "You like me," and almost immediately regret it, as though something as innocuous as *you like me* is a regrettable thing to say. The thing is, I don't really know if he does. I don't really know if I even like him; I have no idea how we feel about each other.

I do know that suddenly I'm nervous.

That high that came from being in a familiar environment, that *wow* I miss, is wearing off, my boldness wearing down with it, because Ezra constantly has me upside down wondering who on Earth I am and what I'm doing.

So I bring us both back into my territory before he can answer. Before he can clarify and make any kind of adjustment to my assumption.

I grab him by the waist and pull him into me, hips flush with mine, and I run my hand up his chest.

Ezra swallows hard and fits one hand around the back of my neck. He slides the other down my waist, fingertips skimming my skin. This. This I can do.

This ground is familiar and here, bodies moving against each other, I know *exactly* how we both feel.

I know exactly what it means when Ezra dips his gaze down to my mouth and then catches himself and looks back at my eyes. Like it requires physical effort. I am comfortable, in the most perfectly hyper-aware, beautifully, desperately *un*comfortable way, when he slides my hair back behind my ear and trails his fingers down the side of my neck. I fight shuddering.

He pulls me in closer and draws his mouth right up next to my ear. I feel it when he whispers, "So this is what you do on Saturday nights."

I say back, voice all low and throaty, "Jealous?"

"A little."

Ezra moves his hips and it's a real surprise that the guy can dance. Not because he's Ezra necessarily, but because he's male, and I can count on one hand the high school boys I know who can actually *dance* with a girl.

But he can. He knows exactly how to move, exactly how to get me to respond so heat is lighting up my stomach, my chest, my thighs. I say, because I need to get a handle on my own train of thought, "This not how you spend your weekends, Holtz?"

He draws back to look at my face and I am sad at the lack of contact, but not at the shadows playing over his jaw, lighting up his cheekbones. That break, that freaking break in his nose. The one that makes him—of all people—look a little dangerous.

He says, "Not typically."

"What do your Saturday nights look like?"

"Havdalah."

I smile. "Yeah, that sounds right."

His almost-grin goes a little dangerous when he says, "And after that?"

I raise an eyebrow.

He answers the begged question: "Textbooks."

"Oooh," I say. I fake a shudder.

His eyebrows pop. "You like that? Algebra equations."

"Talk dirty to me."

He says, low and slow, "Split. Infinitives. Dangling participles. Con-ju-gation."

"Oh god. We're in public."

Ezra smiles, a real one, the kind that I can feel all the way in my knees. He looks so uncharacteristically mischievous when he grins like this. "You wanna fix that?"

"Please," I say. "I thought you wanted to be a deviant for the night."

"And?"

"And we've barely begun to deviate."

He cocks his head, still slowly moving his hips against mine. "You planning on getting me thrown in jail? Or is that not your . . . standard deviation?"

I smirk. "Trying to get me to cuff you already?" I cluck my tongue. "Come inside. Let's find some trouble to get into."

As it turns out, inside, the party is low on trouble. I mean, it's got your standard fare beer, but it's the three-two stuff. No one's even smoking weed. I pretend I'm not disappointed by that, because part of me wants Ezra to think I'm just a little better than I am, but who am I kidding? I was extremely looking forward to lighting up.

It's been *forever.*

It's been forever since I did . . . anything like that, really.

Behind me, someone says, "AMALIA," and I whirl around to find Brent and Sasha. I break into a grin and they get me to come play beer pong with them. Ezra follows.

I destroy; I always do.

I have a reputation to uphold: kills at beer pong, can drink you under the table if she feels like it, more into weed than beer and knows who to score from, deep artiste. I'm mostly operating on all cylinders tonight. The black tank with a kind of gothed out Starry Night on it and the ripped-up skinny jeans do wonders for the artist rep that I still kind of feel like I'm faking, and no one here has weed, so I'm exempt from that (tragically). The beer, though, I can do.

I haven't drunk much, I haven't had to. Like I said, I'm killer at beer pong.

Just enough to be the tiniest bit fuzzy for the next few minutes.

Ezra isn't drinking at all, which is cool—it's always good to have a DD.

I get bored pretty fast, honestly; there's just only so long you can play this kind of stuff before shit starts to blend together like watercolor.

The littlest beginnings of any level of alcohol effect have completely worn off.

I toss the ping-pong ball and it splashes, and then I fall back into Ezra.

He leans over my shoulder and says, lips brushing the shell of my ear, "So this is trouble?"

"What, you disappointed?"

I feel him shrug against my back. "Nah, it's fine. I guess I just thought a night, cut totally loose, with Amalia Yaabez, would be a little wilder than beer pong in a basement. But what do I know?"

I narrow my eyes and turn around. A cheer goes up behind me and Ezra glances over my shoulder. Someone's drinking. "Is that a challenge?"

"Of course it is."

I put my hands on my hips. "If you think you're up for it."

He laughs and I flip off the table, "Later, losers."

Brent takes a long drink and gives me this little salute of a wave. I slide my fingers down Ezra's arm and grab his hand, even though that feels kind of relationship-y. Even though it feels, weirdly, like crossing some sort of barrier that neither of us has vocalized. But I need to lead him through the party and then through the woods, and if that means slipping my fingers through his, so be it.

If it means I am brushing my skin over the lightest roughness of his fingerprints, the harder coarseness of his callouses, if it means I am completely, utterly, *focused* on the pinpoints of every place his palm presses into mine.

Well.

That's just part of the plan.

I tug him along behind me and, to his credit, he doesn't ask me where we're going. He just follows. Like he trusts me. Like he believes I know what I'm doing.

And I guess when it comes to risk-taking behavior, I do.

I follow the little faerie path with him until we hit the hot tub. I can't believe no one's out here, but maybe it's just too warm. Yeah, that's gotta be it. Hot tubs do not sound appealing on this suffocating, damp October night.

Ezra says, "Man, Amalia. You know how to get a guy to safe out."

"No," I say. "Trust, Padawan. I'm not dragging you into a hot tub."

"Thank god."

"WAIT," I say. "SSSHHH." I whisper-yell it, quiet but urgent.

Ezra furrows his brow and I yank him back behind the hot tub.

"What the hell, Amal—"

"Look."

He pops his head up over the hot tub's edge from where we're crouching, and I follow him.

"Is that . . .?" I say.

"Whoa." Ezra looks at me, eyebrows up (some people's eyes are the windows to their soul. Ezra's *eyebrows* are). He says, "Is that . . . Janelle and Lina?"

Janelle's back is against a tree just a few plants deep in the woods behind the hot tub. Her cane (patterned in exactly the same plaid as her wheelchair; I can see now even in the dim, lit only by the lighting in the ground around the hot tub, that it's patterned duct tape, not washi) is leaning up against a nearby tree.

They're making out, like . . . *INTENSELY MAKING OUT.*

I say, "Well this is weird."

"What's weird?"

"It's weird to see people making out and know you had a hand in it. This must be how all matchmakers have felt throughout history: odd. All the time."

Ezra whispers, "So *that's* what's weird then, not ducking behind a hot tub and watching our classmates/experiment subjects stick their tongues down each other's throats?"

I choke and cover it with my hand. Lina's hand slips up Janelle's shirt and I say, "We should—we should go."

I stifle a cackle, and we creep away, back along the path I had originally intended.

It is only now that I realize I still haven't let go of his hand. I just, uh . . . I need the leverage to get him to move with me.

I curl my fingers tighter and pull him just a little farther—just to the edge of Everett's property.

Across the nothing-feet-high fence are neighbors with a pool.

"Shit," says Ezra.

My mouth curls.

"We can't—you want to hop their fence?"

"Yes."

"And what? Jump in their pool?"

"Yes."

Ezra presses his fingers to his forehead and blows out a breath. He adjusts his glasses at me. I don't know why his disapproval sends a flare right through me, but it does, and I giggle.

"We could get shot, Amalia. Or the cops called. Or. I don't know. There are a number of possible futures playing out in my head right now and none of them are good."

"Okay, Doctor Strange," I say. I pull my top off and his nostrils flare. I have to force my face not to react, not to immediately tip into total smugness. But wow. Do I feel smug. Ezra glances down at my chest, this bright pink bra I picked especially because I look *extremely good* in it, and swallows hard. "I know these people. They don't have guns, first of all. Their daughter goes to our school, and I've swum in the pool before."

"That doesn't mean you can swim in it now. Uninvited. At ten p.m."

"Ezra," I say.

"What."

"They're not home. There's no cars in the driveway, and the Johnsons don't park in their garage. Lights are all off."

He blows out a breath. Rakes a hand through his hair. It rests on the back of his neck. He's nervous. Man, I love that he's about to just lose his shit. I love making him nervous.

"They could come back at any second."

"Then we'd better get in now."

"Jesus. Amalia—"

I slide out of my skinnies—well, shimmy out. There's no getting gracefully out of pants this tight. Then I hop over the fence and jump into the Johnsons' pool in my bra and underwear.

Ezra hisses, "Amalia."

I lean my head back and let the water coat all of my hair.

"*Amalia.*"

I dive under the water and do a front flip, then pop up, skin and hair dripping. I smile at him like this is nothing, like it's completely fine and my heart isn't crashing behind my ribcage, pulse threatening to rip right through my veins. It always is. The high of this has never dulled, even for a second. I'm always running through the terrible possibilities and panicking just a little under my skin. I smile, relaxed and confident, at Ezra. But inside it's all adrenaline.

The thing is, that's what makes it fun.

Ezra meets my eyes for several seconds. Then he groans. He pulls his shirt off and steps out of his shorts and then eyes the fence.

"I can't believe I'm doing this."

I wrinkle my nose and I know my smile about covers my entire face.

He hops the fence and sprints into the water, like as soon as he's here, what he's doing will be less risky. Less extremely against the law.

"How you feeling?" I say.

Ezra says, "Pissed."

"Why?"

"I'm going to get arrested."

"Oh come on. I almost never get arrested."

"*Almost?*"

I splash him in the face and the water droplets cling to his glasses. "Oh," he says. "Oh you are dead."

I squeal and he chases after me, because of course that's what I wanted him to do.

I'm a fast swimmer, but he's faster, and he has me around the waist, pressing me against his bare chest, entire expanse of my back touching him. Touching his skin. Holy shit.

I hope he thinks I'm shaking because I'm in the water.

Forget the fact that the water's never cold here and it isn't cold now.

He spins me around to face him and I smirk.

I open my mouth to ask him what he plans to do with me now that he's caught me, but the words stick in my throat.

Headlights.

Coming up the driveway.

Oh my god.

"Ezra," I say.

"SHIT, yes, I saw."

He drops me and we both scramble for the edge of the pool; we have to be out before they get out of their car and hear us splashing, shit, shit, shit.

"We were in there less than two minutes!" I say as I yank myself up the side of the pool.

Ezra gets out with me and says, "Yeah. I deserve this for listening to you; what the hell was I th—"

"Ssshhh," I say.

I look over at the car, the headlights pointed the exact wrong way. And I realize, the same time I watch Ezra realize: we can't hop that fence again. The angle of the driveway has those headlights aimed exactly where we need to run to get back. They'll see us.

"What do we do?" he whispers. He's starting to panic, which, yes, okay, fair, SAME.

We can't just stand here either because eventually they will leave the car, and the shades are open and the second they walk in, it's a straight shot to the pool.

"Wait," says Ezra. "I've got it."

"Where—"

Ezra grabs my wrist and now it's his turn to pull me. Right down the little outdoor-carpeted path toward the little pool house.

"Shit," he says. "It's locked."

"No," I say. I punch in the code and don't even have time to search Ezra's face for the unsettlingly intoxicating approval before he's jerking me inside and shutting the door.

It's dark in here.

The air is thick and it smells like chlorine, and I guess someone could turn on the light but for reasons, well, knownst to us, neither of us does.

He has me pressed against the wall, chest to my chest. Bare skin against my bra. And I am suddenly acutely aware that I'm not in a swimsuit. I'm in a bra. And underwear.

Honestly, it's not like I'm in a thong. If anything, these are boy shorts; they're *less* revealing than any of my bikinis. This bra might have a little push-up action but it's pretty full coverage; I got professionally fitted for it and everything.

It doesn't matter.

How much skin I'm showing is meaningless next to the knowledge that these are the things I wear under my clothes.

Ezra pushes just a little harder against me and the water droplets on his chest wet my skin, my bra; good lord, am I sweating? Probably. It's a thousand degrees in here.

I feel his heartbeat quicken against mine. Hear his sharp intake of breath when I shift my hips so they brush against his thighs. He's just in his underwear, and, weirdly, for all the making out we've done, for all the sluttiness I've felt I've been engaging in, I guess I haven't seen him in these.

Ezra, it turns out, is a boxers guy.

Check that off the getting-to-know-you list.

He leans down by my ear and says, low but not quite in a whisper, "How long do we wait it out in here?"

"You getting antsy, precious?"

He pinches me and I have to cover my mouth so I don't squeal.

I tug on the back of his slightly too-long hair and he grits his teeth.

I say, "Give it ten minutes. . . . Well, wait, can you see through the window?"

"I was too nervous to look."

"They're not spying on us, Jason Bourne. Just look."

He slides to my side and glances out the window, then breathes a curse, and I furrow my brow.

I don't have too long to be confused.

The sliding glass door shuts, which means it was very recently opened.

There is a very definite splash.

Two.

We wait.

Breathe.

Wait what feels like a freaking hour.

No more splashes.

The young screech and male laughter tell me it's Dani and her brother, not their parents, which is good when it comes to like, tangible consequences. But ultimately worse for two reasons: 1) If we come barreling out of the pool house in front of them, who knows *what* rumors will go around at school, and 2) They will not be going to bed at Old Person O' Clock.

I widen my eyes and stare at Ezra.

He stares back at me. Glances out the window again

My eyes are starting to adjust to the light so I can make out more than the barest gray-blue outline of his face.

"Lord," I whisper, leaning my head back against the wooden wall, roughness scratching against my scalp. My hair is sticking to my chest and back.

Ezra leans forward and taps his forehead to the wall over my shoulder. Every bit of him is pressing against every bit of me. His shoulder to my shoulder, hip to my hip. I feel it when he breathes against me, water running down his chest to slip over my stomach.

"Guess we're here for a while," he says against my neck.

Breathes. Against my neck.

I whisper, even though they probably couldn't hear me even if I spoke out loud, "What did you wanna do?"

He waits a beat. Then says, "Deviate."

He runs his teeth along my neck then pulls back and searches my face.

I grin. "Look at you, Ezra Holtz. Criminal as hell."

"Yeah, I'm a real rebel."

"You're asking me to hook up in a pool house neither of us was invited to while the owners are a few feet away."

He swallows hard. I can see it when his Adam's apple moves. I don't know if I actually hear it or if it's just my mind, filling in the sound.

"You're a terrible influence," he says.

"That's what they tell me."

Ezra backs up just a touch, just enough that I'm not at all trapped by him. Not that I really was before, but it's clear that it's intentional. "You okay?" I say.

"Yes," he says.

We're both still whispering. We will be whispering for a while, I think, or we will be getting caught in this tiny little out building on someone else's property.

"I don't want to pressure you," he says. "I want you to have room to breathe."

I slide my teeth across my lip. "*You. You* are worried about pressuring *me.*"

Ezra runs his hand back through his hair. The water droplets on his glasses have finally started to dry, one by one. "Why wouldn't I be? I know what *I* want to do. I don't know what *you* have in mind to fill the time. Like I said, I'm not a fan of question marks. Especially not with, well, this."

"How many times have you had to clear up question marks in situations like this?"

"What you mean is *how many people have I hooked up with*?"

"It's none of my business," I say suddenly, because I'm worried now that he's going to ask me and I don't even know how to answer the question. I know I don't want to because I'm sure my number would be higher than his and, for some stupid, infuriating, totally unfeminist, hypocritical reason, that matters to me. God, I exhaust me.

He says, "If you want to know, I'll tell you, but I don't care about your numbers and honestly I don't want to get into mine. It's more than you think."

I breathe out. I don't even know what he means by *hooking up*. It could mean making out, it could mean like . . . intercourse. It could mean a number of things that . . . I guess don't matter.

I stare right at him. "It's interesting," I say.

"What is?"

"That you're worried about pressuring me when you and I both know that however many people you've fooled around with, I've fooled around with more. That you're not a slut. And I am. Just. That it would even cross your mind that I'm not the one seducing *you*."

He blinks. Then stares at me hard. He slides his hand over my jaw, up my face. "You're not a slut."

"I am. According to *everyone*, I am."

"So the fuck what?"

I blink hard and just look. Just wait a breath. I don't think I've ever heard him drop an f-bomb. "No," I say. "I know." And I know. I *know*. I wouldn't think this about anyone else. I wouldn't be surprised that a boy wanted explicit confirmation before he tried anything with *any* of my friends who like to fuck around. I would *expect* it. I would *demand* it.

But with me.

With yourself.

Suddenly everything is harder.

"Of course I know," I say. "I'm sorry."

"Why are you sorry?"

"I'm tired. That's a better adjective. Strike and replace."

He backs up a pace. "Okay." He does an incredible job of masking the disappointment in his voice so it sounds almost neutral. Casual. How it sounds, more than anything, is genuine. I hear, then, what I said, and how he's misinterpreted it. He thinks I'm putting a stop to things, and while he's wrong, it's . . . nice. Nice to know that it really would be *okay*. If I were.

Which, well.

I am most definitely, *definitely* not.

"No, no. Come back here."

Ezra gives me a wry look. Quirks his eyebrow so it disappears under his hair.

"Put your hands back on me," I say.

He smirks. And take a step forward. Links his finger in my boy shorts.

I say, "I am tired. Of believing one thing about everyone else and another about myself. I'm tired of people calling me a slut. Like liking sex is a bad thing. But Jesus *Christ—*"

He hisses, "Sssshhhh," and I lower my voice.

"Jesus Christ. A lot of people like sex. What's supposed to happen? We turn eighteen and suddenly at the stroke of midnight, everything below the waist turns on?"

Ezra laughs, low and close to me. Quiet. Controlled.

"Maybe I am a slut."

"Amal—"

"No," I whisper. "Maybe I am." I smile. I actually smile at him brightly. And what do you know? I mean it. I say,

"And you should. You should obviously ask me what I want you to do."

Ezra blows out a breath. He's shaking, his *breath* is shaking.

"Amalia," he says. "What do you want me to do?"

He's looking at me like I am the only thing that exists. Like we can't hear two people just outside these tiny rickety walls splashing in the pool.

I slip my hands behind his back and pull him into me. His hipbones jab into me and it almost hurts. I say, "I want you to touch me. With your hands."

"Where?"

"Anywhere."

I smile and his nostrils flare again and god, the power is *good*.

He leans over me again, one hand on the wall over my shoulder, the other still linked in my underwear, knuckle brushing my hipbone. He kisses me slowly, intentionally, *precisely*. Everything, every shift of his jaw, every movement of his tongue, every breath, every twitch of his fingers, is on purpose.

Ezra kisses me with a plan.

God.

I pull back to breathe and say, so only he can hear me, "What do *you* want to do, Ezra Holtz?"

He says, "Touch you. With my hands."

I say, grinning, "Where?"

Before he kisses me again, he says, "Anywhere," and slides his fingers all the way inside my underwear.

Someone splashes outside.

The moonlight streams in through the window, lights up Ezra's hair, the planes on his face. I shut my eyes and lean my weight against the wall as Ezra dips down to fix the height difference between us.

I never quite realized how much taller he is than me.

I realize it now.

I'm realizing *everything* now.

The hard, lean musculature of his arms, the intense way he kisses me when he's utterly focused, that constant characteristic precision that comes in . . . very *very* handy, it turns out, when applied to his hands—good *lord.*

I dig my fingers into his shoulder and he asks, low and up against my ear, if there's anything I want. Anything that would make it better.

"Just—what you're doing. Is good." I make a little noise in the back of my throat, on accident, when he shifts his hand, and his mouth curls into a grin.

"Ssshhh," he says.

I bite my lip. Hard. Hard enough to mute what things would usually sound like right about now if I weren't trapped trespassing in a tiny, non-insulated building feet away from my classmates.

Suddenly it seems like it would have been a better idea to wait it out in here, *not* hooking up against the wall. Suddenly it occurs to me, both of us breathing what feels like too loud, slipping just a little against the wood and the slick concrete floor, trying like hell to keep my voice *out of this, dammit,* that it would have been the safe play to just sit here and talk.

But well.

Who ever got a great story out of the safe play?

Not that this is something I can exactly tell my grand-kids about.

Ezra scrapes his teeth over my neck and everything crests over me. I bury my face in his chest and make that same little noise into it, muffled by his skin.

I think: *There is nothing wrong with how I feel right now.*

There is nothing wrong with liking this.

My god, this guy smells amazing—is it his deodorant? Or am I just high off this whole night?

I think: *It is worth it. To be called a slut. If all that means is that I am doing the things that I want.*

I want a lot of things.

Right now, being trapped in this pool house, screwing around with Ezra Holtz, is what I want the most.

CHAPTER TWENTY-ONE

Psychological Symptoms Of Being In Love

-or-

How Being In Love Can Sometimes Feel Exactly Like Fasting On Religious Holidays

‹use as possible evaluative tool on reports›

1. *Focus on the positives*

2. *Inability to banish some obsessive thinking*

3. *Emotional instability*

4. *Intense emotional connection and intimacy*

5. *Realignment of priorities*

Yom Kippur is like the holiest day on the Jewish calendar. Well, technically there is an argument to be made—and nine bajillion *have* been made—for Shabbat being the holiest. Or Purim, actually. I don't know; Ezra probably has a very definite, four-hour-long opinion on it. I make a mental note never to ask him.

But Shabbat happens every Saturday, and on Purim you're supposed to celebrate and get totally drunk, so Yom Kippur just kind of *feels* holier as holy days go?

No matter where you fall on that argument, it's definitely one of the Big Ones. Like, if the Big Ones to a bunch of people are Christmas and Easter? Those are the ones that people give you time off for and come home for and all of that? Well, Rosh Hashanah and Yom Kippur and Passover—those are our Big Ones.

Now. I'm extremely not saying that it's Jewish Christmas (neither is Chanukah), and it's not Jewish Easter—because we don't have those. That's like saying that mushrooms are vegan veal or something, which is stupid because vegans don't have veal. They're not. Chanukah is Jewish Chanukah and Yom Kippur is Jewish Yom Kippur and Rosh Hashanah is Jewish Rosh Hashanah.

The End.

I'm just saying . . . they're some of the ones that are extra holy, extra important, the ones that a lot of people go the extra mile to make extra holiday-y.

Rosh Hashanah we already did ten days ago. Passover isn't until Spring. Yom Kippur is today. And by today, I mean last night, because that's how we do it on Ye Olde Jewish Calendarre. We go from sundown to sundown.

Last night was Kol Nidre. It's always my favorite because it's more beautiful, more reverent, more *haunting*. The special melodies the cantor sings, the prayers that have this extra layer of gravity, of finality. It's serious. It's . . . I don't know. Moving, I guess.

I don't know that I'd call myself much of a spiritual person. Kind of? I kind of, sort of am. But it's not something that usually matters really deeply to me, when it comes down to it. Not the way, like, painting does. My culture matters to me. Tradition matters to me, sometimes. The spiritual part of it, I usually feel the least.

But not on Yom Kippur.

Especially not on Kol Nidre.

This is the time that it always, *always* matters to me for some reason. That I feel things in my chest. That I actually *feel* the melodies and mean every word of every prayer. For me, today always feels significant, feels like for some reason, the religion itself is stitched into my bones.

Kol Nidre is over, and today is the rest of it, which means that we are in synagogue almost all day. Mom and Dad had to fight again to get Kaylee's and my absences excused, because everyone is an asshole, but either way, here I am.

Temple is totally packed; it's always packed on the high holidays. I like it, how full it feels today.

The cantor starts reciting "Ashamnu" in his rich baritone and goose bumps pop up all over my skin. I smile over at Ben, and I am starving to death and my stomach hurts and we are singing the world's most upbeat, catchiest song about like, ten billion sins we have committed during the year, but I am happy.

I'm just.

Happy.

Kaylee is singing about a half a note off the whole time, loudly in my ear, and that is tradition, so it doesn't bug me. I love all of this.

The focus on repentance, on forgiveness, on acknowledging how deeply you really do screw up during the year and how there is always the chance to do better next year. To become a better person. This whole season, from Rosh Hashanah until now, is about becoming better. About seeking forgiveness from people you've wronged. Granting forgiveness to those who have asked it of you and tried to fix it. About doing tzedakah. Making the world better for everyone else. For you. About becoming the best version of you that you can possibly be. And about knowing that next year when you fall short, you can fix it all again.

Like I said, something about today makes me *feel it* in a way that sometimes I don't.

The cantor sings about how on Rosh Hashanah our fates are written, and today, on Yom Kippur, they are sealed. It always gives me chills, even though I don't know that I'm that superstitious about it all.

Standing here with my family, praying, feeling the pangs of hunger twist my stomach and thirst drying out my mouth, standing and sitting and watching the sunlight stream in through the stained glass windows of the synagogue, I feel.

Glad.

Content.

Fulfilled.

The service lets out, and we have a couple hours to kill until *ne'ilah*.

I think we're gonna hang around temple because we live too far away to justify going back home and today is a fast day so it's not like we're gonna go out to a late lunch or something.

We wander around as a unit, trying to find something to do; there's a couple of like, social justicey things going between services—people from the community talking about social issues around the city. Some guided meditation stuff. Yom Kippury things to do that aren't actual services for people like us who don't want to have to leave and come back but who also do want to stick around for ne'ilah, the last service of the day.

I find myself reading names on the walls here and there. Looking at little art pieces put up by some of the kids at the day school (which we've never been able to afford. Like, el oh el there's three of us; public school was the only option there).

I find my attention wandering.

I find myself . . . looking for Ezra Holtz.

Here is the unsettling thing about that: I am absolutely not looking for him so that we can hook up. I have zero dirty thoughts in my brain. Well, okay, let's not get ridiculous; I have zero *specifically directed at Ezra at this moment in time* dirty thoughts in my brain. I have no plans to sneak off to some unoccupied area on the grounds and do terrible things to him. I can't. Fasting on Yom Kippur means fasting from a lot of things. We don't eat, we don't drink—not even water. Nothing. No deodorant. No washing your face. And BEST of all: no sexy things. You are totally not allowed to bang on Yom Kippur.

I have no intention of breaking that particular rule today, and I am absolutely *positive* that even if I did, Ezra doesn't. So what's happening here is: I am looking for Ezra Holtz.

And I have no idea why.

Before I can really think through the implications of that, Ezra is bumping into my shoulder with his.

He says, "Hey, stranger." His eyes are glittering. He's so relaxed, like he knows me, like he's comfortable, like we're friends or something and hahaha I'm panicking.

"Hey," I say.

I'm weird and stiff.

I know I'm weird and stiff. I'm hoping it just comes off as hungry.

"How you holding up?"

I shrug. "Probably about as well as you are."

"Yeah?"

"I want to eat my hand. Or my forearm; it's meatier."

He laughs, shoulders dropped, one hand in a pocket, the other adjusting his kippah. "You're fasting today?"

I scoff at him. "Yes."

He holds his hands up in a surrender and says, "No judgment either way, I'm just surprised."

And yeah, sure. I'm not super observant when it comes down to it; he knows that. And not everyone fasts today. Some people can't, for health reasons, which is totally fine. Some people can but choose not to, and hey, whatever, that's fine, too. None of my business either way; people observe in whatever way makes the most sense to them. But I'm a little annoyed that he would assume.

Not for long; it's just a twinge, one I'm used to with him. It dissipates about as quickly as it came and I just say, "There are a number of things about me that might surprise you, Holtz."

He raises an eyebrow and shifts just the slightest bit closer to me. Slight enough that were I not constantly, *constantly* aware of every way he moves, every little breath and facial tic, I wouldn't even notice it, I don't think. I doubt anyone else passing by notices the half-inch difference when he leans toward me. No one else can taste the sudden dryness in my mouth (well, sudden INCREASE in dryness) or the jump in my pulse.

He says, "It's usually the dehydration that kills me. Way worse than the not eating."

"Honestly," I say. "Hope you slammed your Gatorade yesterday."

"Please," he says, "do I look like this is my first day?"

I smile, wide and relaxed, and I am so unsettled that I am enjoying this so much. If the rabbi passes by, he'll wonder if we're apologizing to one another for a whole year's worth of transgressions and trying to swallow the idea of forgiveness. He'll chuckle and roll his eyes and quicken his pace so he doesn't get wrapped up in another ridiculous rivalrous discussion that will eventually devolve into barbs and fury.

"How's your day going?"

"It's good," he says. "People make jokes about how this is no one's favorite holiday, because it's serious and you're hungry. You don't get to get wasted like on Purim—"

"Or Passover."

"Yeah, WOW, first time I ever got drunk was on glass number two of Manischewitz at a seder when I was thirteen and holy–anyway." He coughs. "Anyway."

"As you were saying, you alcoholic."

He narrows his eyes. "As though you were the model of restraint at your first seder as an adult."

"Of course I wasn't. But I'm Amalia Yaabez." I blow my hair out of my eyes and strike a dramatic pose, overly edgy, silly. I don't know if it's the lack of calories making me lightheaded and goofy or if it's the hormones and Ezra, but it's something. And I feel light and fun and free.

Ezra laughs. I want to keep it in my pocket.

He says, "I can't argue with that point."

I say, "Are you ever going to finish your story?"

"Right," he says. "Right." He looks just a little caught off guard, the smallest bit off balance. He's fiddling too intently with his kippah and it's dangerous how much I love that he's never like this. That I only see him this way–sometimes–with me. "Anyway, I guess I'm weird–"

"That's the truth."

He smirks the slightest bit, then rolls his eyes. "I *guess I'm weird*, because I've always loved today. The whole process."

"No," I say, "me too, actually."

"Yeah?" His eyes light up. In surprise, in camaraderie, delight? Something makes them pretty.

"Yeah. Even the crappy parts."

"The crappy parts are what make it so meaningful."

"Part of it, anyway."

"Part of it," he agrees.

"Plus," I say, "what food tastes better than whatever you break your fast with in . . . what? Five hours?"

He glances down at his watch because of course Ezra, biggest dork of the century, wears a wristwatch. "Five hours and eleven minutes."

"Man, you're a nerd," I say.

"I'm just hungry."

"Wow are those two things not mutually exclusive."

He purses his lips and says, "First chametz after Passover."

"Hm?"

"The only food that tastes better than whatever we're gonna eat in five hours. That first cookie after eight days of matzah and protein? Tough to beat."

I blow out a low whistle and say, "I don't even know how to choose. Tell me what you're going to eat tonight."

He shrugs a shoulder. "Anything. Where are you going?"

"Mexican, I think."

"Maybe—" He cuts himself off and that hand is on his kippah again.

"Spit it out, Holtz."

"Maybe I'm doing Mexican?"

I meet his eyes, and it feels like we're talking about more than what we're going to eat tonight. It feels like we're asking each other eight thousand terrifying questions that neither of us really knows how to ask *or* to answer. Maybe we'll . . . maybe we'll disappear after dinner or something and hook up. I'm sure that's why. I'm sure that's what he's thinking. I find myself saying, "Right after ne'ilah, the little place without a sign down the road."

"Yeah, I know it. What are the odds that that's where I suddenly recall us thinking about going."

"It would be so random," I say, smiling and nervous all at once, "if I happened to see you there."

Ben suddenly comes up beside me and glances at Ezra, and to his credit, his face betrays very little.

He says, "Ezra," and Ezra says, "Ben. How're you doing?"

"Fine."

Ezra nods, that pleasant non-smile on his face. I never noticed how his eyes smile even when his mouth doesn't.

Ben turns immediately to me and says, "We're going to the guided meditation thing. You coming?"

"Yeah," I say. "I'll go." I turn to Ezra, and it's stupid how hopeful my voice sounds when I say, "I'll see you?"

Ezra scrapes his teeth over his lip, catches it for just a half second. He says, "I'll see you."

CHAPTER TWENTY-TWO

**TEST GROUP
ARIEL AND CARLOS**

 SUBJ. LINE: RESIGNING. SORRY.

SENDER: Carlos Acevedo

CONTENT OF E-MAIL: So, listen. This shit is not working out. Thanks for trying, I guess? But we are just fundamentally incompatible. If anything, this experiment did nothing but screw us up. Not that we were destined to be friends or something (No. Way. On earth.) but we could stand hanging out like, tangentially before. We could cross paths without wanting to strangle each other.

I'm into a good, old-fashioned hate make out like anyone else, but this is not that, it's never going to be that, and last night we tried to grit our teeth past all this shit and make it through your last set of questions but she walked out.

Good thing. I was going to walk out if she didn't.

To put it delicately, I fucking hate her. To put it scientifically, it's mutual. I'm not going into why because I don't think you guys need that for any reason; we're just REALLY DIFFERENT and not in a good way. The end.

So. Thanks, or something. But I am out.

When September bleeds into October, and the summer hasn't quite died yet—welcome to the south where summer never dies; at most, it has a brief coma—Skylar's house starts to feel like a concentration of Halloween. Leaves litter the walkway up to her porch stoop and the wind feels just a little ominous, and I don't know if I love it or hate it.

She invited me over and of course I came because I honestly cannot tell her that I'm afraid of her cool, haunted-looking house, so obviously I'm here.

I just want to say, in my defense, that someone *did* die here like a hundred years ago and sometimes at night, the lights flicker.

Skylar and I are hanging out in her backyard, which is sort of creepy in a Haunted Mansion kind of way, but not in a "What if I get locked away in one of these creaky rooms with a vengeful ghost" claustrophobic kind of way, so it's fine.

She has an old swing set back here that her nephews sometimes use, and we're swinging back and forth, back and forth with the wind.

She says, suddenly, into the quiet, "Amalia?"

"Sky?"

"I miss you."

A frown flickers across my face. "I'm right here."

She's quiet. Skylar is usually a little quiet, so by itself, that's okay. This kind of quiet, though, it feels like the breath before something big. Feels like waiting. It makes me nervous. I pump my legs harder so I can fly into the air, high enough that my hair flies behind me and catches wind.

I glance over at Skylar and she's just barely swinging back and forth, barely moving, so I breathe. And I allow gravity to take me back down to earth.

Skylar says, when I'm even with her again, "Then why do I miss you?"

I say, and it's a lie, "I don't know."

Skylar looks at me, really looks at me, and I can't lie to her. Not to her wide blue eyes and serious, intense face that I never, never lie to. Suddenly there's a pit and a knot in my stomach all at once. It's painfully empty and terribly twisted. I feel guilty for keeping secrets from her, even though they're mine and I don't owe them to anyone.

It doesn't matter.

Keeping secrets this big from Skylar feels a whole lot like lying.

I say, and it comes out a whisper that almost gets swallowed by the breeze: "I didn't get into art school."

Skylar blinks, holds onto the swing, and says, "I'm sorry, what?"

"I didn't—" I choke a little. It hurts: my pride, my conscience, my everything. To tell her out loud, now, after lying to her about this big deal in my life for months.

When I've never not told her something this big, when she's never not told me something this big. Not since the ninth grade. "I didn't get in. To any of them."

Skylar kind of coughs. She stares out at her big, tree-laden backyard. She looks back at me. "Why didn't you tell me?"

I shrug. "I just." I want to say *It didn't seem important. I forgot. It's not like it involves you.* But none of those are the reason. The reason I didn't tell her is because: "I was embarrassed."

She recoils. Like I hit her or something. "Embarrassed?" She blinks. Processing it. "*Embarrassed?* What did you think I was going to do? Did you think I was going to laugh at you or something? That sucks! You didn't get into art school! What the *hell?*"

I swallow down the giant lump in my throat and say, "Of course I was embarrassed! You're going to a conservatory! You're an amazing bassist and you're going to play with a symphony or something and your perfect girlfriend is gonna go off and be a singer and both of you have everything you ever wanted, and then there's me. A fucking failure."

"Amalia."

"No," I say. I'm blinking back tears. "You know it's true. It's always been true."

Skylar says, "I have *never* thought of you as a failure. I'm hurt. That you didn't tell me. I could never keep something that huge from you, oh my god. But you're not—you're not a failure. You say I have everything I ever wanted but, Amalia! I've always wished I could be care-free like you. Cutting class and having adventures because you want to have them and making out with people and doing *whatever else* with them because you want to? You're going to bounce back from this and go off and live some cool, whirling, twirling, kickass free life and I'm going to be closed in my room with my bass."

"GODDAMMIT," I say, and Skylar stops swinging. Just digs her feet into the earth and stares at me, wide-eyed. "This!" I say. "This is exactly why I couldn't tell you."

"Because I'm trying to encourage you?"

"Because you're trying to fix it! You're trying to fix everything by making yourself tiny. By making yourself nothing, so I'll feel amazing in comparison to you. Because you feel like the only way I could possibly feel good about who I am and what I've accomplished is if you play yourself down. What the hell does that say about how you see me?"

"That's not fair."

I throw my hands in the air. "How? How is it not fair? It's always been this way. Always, always. You being amazing and thinking I'm some novelty of a person or something because I'm *wild* and *fun* and then trying to make me feel better for being a fuck-up by saying shit like this. It's exhausting." I hear myself being mad, hear myself suddenly being furious and acting like a jerk, and I take five seconds to breathe. To try not to take all of this out on her—all my disappointment, all my insecurities, all the things that made it hard to be with her years ago and sometimes make it hard to be her best friend now. It's always been kind of hard with us and I don't know whose fault it is, or if it's anyone's, but we tried this the romantic way, and we have been doing this the platonic way, and sometimes it turns out *every* way is wrong with someone. I am hurt, I think, because hearing her say things this way confirms that whole manic pixie theory of mine. That when we broke up, I felt like this, and that even now, even as her friend, her *best* friend, she still sees me that way. A force. Without real problems. *Fun.* Fun who leaves.

I say, quieter, more gently, consciously trying not to be a total ass: "I'm sorry. That's not—that's not what you're trying to do. I'm just . . . it's hard. To watch you. To watch Ellie. Get all these things, like you always have, and here I am. The person who's going to bounce back from everything. But maybe I won't. I shouldn't be keeping my life from you, okay? And I shouldn't . . . I shouldn't blame you for all my multitudes of shit. But you're so. So freaking perfect, Skylar." I don't even look at her; I'm wiping at my eyeliner because of course I didn't wear waterproof eyeliner today.

She says, "You're being a jerk, Amalia."

"I know."

"You can't put this on me. I can't believe you didn't tell me."

I'm crying more. I can't believe I didn't tell her either. But I just—I just couldn't. I say, "I'm also hooking up with Ezra Holtz."

She says, "*What?*"

I shrug.

"For how long?"

"Not long," I say.

"Have you guys had sex?"

I shrug again and say, "With hands."

She says, "Jesus. You didn't tell me *that* either?"

I look up at the sky and twist the ropes, let myself spin a little. Then I let go. I'm not twisted enough to get totally out of control but enough that the momentum will take me away. Will allow me to give up control of the swing, of where exactly I am going.

"Am I even your best friend, Amalia?" I hear the sniffling in her voice and I hate it. *I hate it* when she cries.

"Yes," I say without a thought. "You are. Of course you are. You just . . . it's difficult, sometimes, being best friends with a person who's so much better than you are."

"I'm not better than you," she says. Mumbles, almost.

"You're a musician. You get good grades. You're smart and nice and cool and you're not a slut who people whisper about in the hallways. You're not just *wildness*. Like— like I am. You're Good. You wouldn't hook up with a boy illicitly when you didn't even want to hang out with him. You wouldn't sleep with someone you're not in love with, and I sure have."

"So what?" she says. "You think that makes either of us better than the other? Because we live different lives? People might call you a slut, but those people are assholes and they're the same people who call me a prude. Well. A prude AND a slut because I'm bisexual, so I have to be both, obviously."

My mouth tips up. "Obviously."

Skylar runs her hand through her long hair. She says, "You used to tell me everything."

I whisper, "I'm sorry."

"I don't want you to look at me and see all the things you aren't. I love you. I love you and you're not me and you shouldn't want to be."

224

"I know." I'm crying again. Like, really stupid hard. It's embarrassing. "I know."

Skylar. Good, Sweet Skylar, is hugging me even though I was a jerk to her and said some things I'll probably regret later, but she's hugging me and making soothing noises and I don't think I deserve her.

We go inside.

We watch a movie.

Just her and me.

It's normal, without this big secret I don't even know why I kept between us.

But I don't know.

After everything I said, I guess . . . it feels like there's a distance there. That I'm not at arm's length, but then when we fall asleep, I need to keep just a few inches away. Like there's a quiet little barrier there, now that she knows all these tangled things I've been feeling and keeping from her.

She passes out before I do and I wonder if I'm making everything up.

If this is all in my head.

I don't think it is.

CHAPTER TWENTY-THREE

TEST GROUP
SAM AND RILEY

Sam: So hey

Riley: So hey

Sam: I miss you

Riley: what a coincidence

Riley: im waiting by your front door

Sam: Are you really??

Riley: nah, but I could be

Sam: come

Riley: you remember what we said, right?
What we decided? You weren't too
drunk?

Sam: Nah, Ri, I remember. I don't . . .
I don't think I want to make out
with you either

Riley: Yeah

Riley: Okay

Sam: Would it be weird if I said I loved you though? I'm doing this over text because it's weird in person

Riley: Uh. I mean. Well . . .

Sam: Like I love you a lot.

Sam: It hasn't been that long since we started to get to know each other so I know it's weird

Sam: And I don't mean the way we were supposed to like . . . fall in love or whatever?

Riley: Ok?

Sam: I just mean that like . . . like ok. When I showed up at your house last week and your mom was being a shit to you and your dad . . . yeah. I wanted to take you to the amusement park and ride rides and whatever and get you OUT OF THERE. WITH ME. Whatever it took.

Riley: Is that why you told me you had an emergency, then we wound up on a roller coaster?

Sam: yeah

Sam: Sorry?

Riley: No.

Riley: Thank you

Sam: That's how I love you

Riley: Were you gonna win me a stuffed
animal if I'd let you?

Sam: Yeah. But like a big scary-ass one

Riley: sounds romantic

Sam: It's not

Riley: lol

Riley: same

Sam: I love you like you're my friend, you're
like. Like a BEST friend. Already? Idk
it sounds stupid.

Sam: Fuck am I drunk again

Sam: I just mean like how people say,
"Dude I totally love you!" Like I'm
glad ur in my life or whatever. I guess.

Sam: Wait same like it's not romantic or same
like "Dude you totally love me!" too

Riley: both

Sam: ok

Riley: ok

Riley: Im coming over

Sam: im kind of drunk

Riley: good I bet you'll agree to watch the
actually GOOD star wars way easier then

Sam: dumb little bears

Riley: they're great little bears

Riley: im coming over

Sam: ok

Sam: bring bears wars

I am home before anyone wakes up.

Leaving Skylar's house this time felt like an escape, rather than something to be disappointed about. Not that either of us was being mean to each other. Not that there's anything explicitly *wrong*, even. We just . . . we both know the energy is different. That if we are being honest with ourselves, it's been slowly becoming different for a while.

It's kind of like how it was back when we broke up. After the first couple weeks, when we both realized we actually *did* want to stay friends, that we were the only two people in history who have actually meant that, well, it was weird, still. Adjusting, figuring out how to be around each other without wanting to make out.

It worked, eventually. I haven't wanted to kiss her in years. She is one hundred percent my friend. And I am certain it's mutual.

But now it's like things are changing again, and this time is sadder. This time isn't going from one good relationship type to another equally good one. It's going from friendship to . . . well.

I don't want to think about it.

All I know, all I can acknowledge in my own head is that it's different and it feels like losing something and maybe I'm not as sad about it as I should be. And maybe that makes me kind of a bitch. Maybe it doesn't.

What it definitely makes me is leaving early.

Skylar, for her part, seems fine with the sunrise departure.

I am alone with the quiet in the house for a good half hour before Ben comes down the stairs.

"You're up early."

He shrugs. "Studying to do, sis."

I furrow my brow. Good lord, is *everyone* in this house suddenly becoming a nerd? If even Ben can fall, there's no hope of me making a recovery. "Studying."

He scoffs and flicks me on the forehead, then slides into a chair at the kitchen table and takes my full cup of coffee. "Yeah, ass. I'm doing an apprenticeship? If you recall?"

"Right," I say. "But—you have to study for that?"

"Christ. You've been hanging around that Holtz kid too much; you're grounded. Yeah, I have to study. Gonna have to get my electrical license eventually. Plus, you think I'm just gonna nail all that electrical code without looking at it every once in a while? The book's like a thousand pages long."

I would spit out my coffee if he wasn't drinking it.

"Yeahhhhh," he says, smiling and gloating. "Do I need to study for that. If I don't wanna be electrocuted, I should pay attention sometimes."

"No, right, sorry. Duh. I just thought not having to study shit was kind of one of the biggest benefits of doing a trade."

He rolls his eyes and kicks his feet up on the chair across the table. "No. The benefit is getting paid to learn shit."

"Point in your favor." I look at the wood grain of the table. Run my fingers over it, suddenly thinking about the composition, all the chemistry involved in holding this solid together under my fingers. I say, "Do you like it?"

Ben says, "Like what?"

"Electricking."

"Yeah, that's what they call it."

"Shut up."

"I do, though."

"Yeah?"

He takes a long swallow. "That so weird?"

"No," I say. "I just—you never wanted to do that before. I'd always kind of thought it was maybe a temporary thing until you figured it out."

He says, "It kind of was, at first. I didn't know what I wanted to do and I sure as hell wasn't about to drop ten grand a semester to not figure it out. But then, I don't know, I wound up liking it. I like working with my hands. I like the challenge, every day, figuring out how to fix these problems that no one else knows how to do. I like the guys I work with. I like the *money*."

I laugh.

"Plumbing makes more but I don't want to deal with all the . . . shit." He frames his smile in this cheesy pun exaggeration and I'm laughing but shaking my head.

"It's weird," I say, "the way things work."

"Seems like you're saying more than you're saying."

In the breath between his suggesting that and my answering, Mom walks in.

"You're home early."

"Mmhmm," I say.

She doesn't press. Mom isn't a person to pry, and it's one of the best things about her. She just waits. Trusts you to tell her if you need to.

She says, "Coffee?"

Ben says, "Nah, Amalia made me some."

I scowl and say, "Please."

Mom's mouth curls and she heads to the coffee maker.

I look back at Ben. "I—you know it's so weird, but I actually really like chemistry?"

He whisper-yells, "Neeeeeerd."

I hit him and Mom says, still facing the coffee pot as the water heats, "Go for the throat, baby, whose daughter are you?"

I say, "I honestly might major in it. I can't believe it but I might?"

"What about your art?" Mom says.

I shrug. I say, "I don't know."

Mom says, "You don't have to."

"I might restore art. I'd need chemistry to do that anyway. That would be kind of cool, right? Maybe not. I don't . . . I guess I don't know, but I didn't know I would be the kind of person who liked science before and I was wrong about that, so."

"So, I'm right," Mom says. The coffee starts dripping into the pot.

"Hmm?"

"I'm right. You don't have to know."

"Ugh," I say.

Ben says, "Moms, man."

Mom singsongs, "My life is a blessing to my children," and brings me a mug.

This morning, things feels slow and warm and . . . stressful in one way.

But despite everything, they don't feel dire.

It feels like . . . like everything has a prayer of being okay.

I spend the next week poring over chemistry textbooks, feeling bad for ignoring more smoker's corner texts until they stop coming, and a little bad that I don't even get any at all from my Cooler Friends. But I'm busy anyway. I don't have time. Not for them, not for Skylar, not for anything but freaking academia.

Sukkot comes and Ezra wants to know if I want to come hang out in the sukkah he built with his own two hands because of course he did. Of course he totally overachieved.

A sukkah is this temporary structure you build for Sukkot, and you spend a ton of time in it theoretically. You eat in it, read in it, hang out in it, whatever. Until the holiday is over. Our synagogue built one like they do every year, but Ezra actually built his own, and I don't know why it surprises me except that I've never actually been in, like, a personal one.

Of course, I go over to his house.

I am unsettled, deeply, by how much I'm looking forward to getting there.

I pull up in his driveway and go to knock on his door, but he pulls it open.

Because, what? He was waiting for me?

Well. Who could blame him, I guess. We have been having a hell of a time together. It's been . . . fun. Mouths and hands and skin type fun.

I'd be waiting for me, too.

He says, "Come on," and we walk back through his house into his backyard. There's a structure, wood-framed on three sides, draped with canvas. Woven through the roof are little vines, so the whole thing looks . . . magical. It's not expertly put-together, exactly. Even from here, I can see the uneven joints, the places where the wood frame has splintered just a little from an imperfect hammering job. But that kind of makes it better—less manufactured. It looks like he *cared*.

This is how Ezra is.

About everything.

He leads me to it with a bright smile in his eyes, and then he turns around. He sweeps his arm behind him and puts on an affected academic voice, and says, "Step into my sukkah."

"Okay, professor."

"You should see me in tweed."

"God," I say, rolling my eyes and stepping past him into the little house. "You *would* own tweed."

He snorts, and I can't see it because he's behind me, but I imagine him smiling and that's enough to send downright dangerous warmth through my stomach.

I pull out a little folding chair from where it's situated around an equally cheap folding table and say, "You built this?"

"Sure did."

"With your own hands."

He holds his hands out, palms up, and I can see the scratches on them. Where the cheap wood splintered and dug into his fingers, his palms, a couple scratches up his forearms. I cross my legs because something about it is ridiculously hot, I can't help it.

"Impressed, Yaabez?" he says with a smirk.

"Don't get cocky."

"Too late."

I groan. "I thought I told you not to last-name me. It sounds weird in your mouth."

"I thought you liked my mouth."

I cough and he looks instantly *extremely* pleased with himself. Because I really am enjoying spending time with him, talking with him, I say, "Only when it's not talking."

I can't quite interpret the look on his face. It's amused, but also . . . I don't know. His brow is drawn in just a little too tight, eyes not quite smiling. He almost looks hurt?

Which can't be right.

I decide I'm imagining it when he says, "That makes two of us."

I let out a breath. "So," I say, "you bring all the pretty girls out here?"

"No," he says. "Just you."

And suddenly that tightness is back in my chest.

"Really?"

"Yes."

A muscle twitches in his jaw, and his fingers are moving to smooth away nothing on the table. He says, "I've kind of been wanting to talk to y—"

And I talk over him to say, "A sukkah is a strange spot to start a seduction."

He stops talking. Rolls his eyes. "I'm not always trying to seduce you. *Step into my sukkah*, in retrospect, was maybe not my best move anyway."

I laugh. "Eh. Well. It'll work on me."

"Yeah?"

"Why else would I have come over?"

He raises an eyebrow.

"It's not like you asked me to come over because we're friends, Holtz."

He blinks. Takes a second while another unreadable looks flashes over his face. Then says, "Right." He looks at me. *Peers* at me. "Right."

"Sure is fun to fool around, though."

He's back to cocky in a blink. "That I cannot argue with."

My gaze dips down to his collarbone, to his hands all scratched up and calloused. I say, "Your parents home?"

His mouth curls. "Not for hours."

I stand and cock my head toward the house. "Well then. You want to show me that tweed collection?"

CHAPTER TWENTY-FOUR

TEST GROUP
JANELLE AND LINA

 INT: *Car. Black cloth seats, vehicle is pretty small. Unclear what make and model. Front seat, camera is clearly braced on the dashboard. Lina sits in the front seat, hair in big bouncing curls, lips a brilliant red. Janelle leans back in the passenger's seat, in a pretty purple and blue headscarf. She has a soft smile on her lips.*

Lina: *We'll get you the full report, the questionnaire for your data?*

Janelle: *Mine's already filled out, but slacker here—*

Lina, shoving Janelle, eyes sparkling: *Shut up.*

Janelle: *Finish up this recording and I will.*

Even through the screen, Lina's immediate blush is obvious.

Lina: *I was . . . we were both nervous about jumping into that last set of questions. It's a little like ripping your heart open for someone, isn't it? Answering questions about your deepest pains, your biggest dreams, the only memory you wish you could erase, the only one you would save if you had to let every one go but one? That's . . . that's not. It's not easy.*

Janelle starts playing with the ends of Lina's hair.

Janelle: *I just . . .*

Janelle turns to Lina, and Lina stops looking in the camera to stare back at Janelle.

Janelle: *I feel like I know you better than I should. And like . . . like I feel more for you than I should? But I swear, Lina, I feel like I'm in love with you. And—*

Janelle darts her eyes to the camera.

Janelle: *Turn that off?*

Lina, grinning at the camera: *We'll get you those evaluations.*

End recording.

238

Ezra smirks, this self-assured, obviously sexual thing. I am comfortable again. It's a pattern, I guess, now. But one I wove all on my own, one I am happy to continue weaving.

I take it as a yes and move past him to leave the sukkah and sneak into his house. Well, not *sneak* exactly; there's no one home. But it's rule-breaking and that feels sneaky anyway.

I feel fingers on the crook of my elbow. Gentle pressure.

I turn around and Ezra tightens his hand, cocky smile curving up just a little higher, crooked as the break in his nose.

He says, "Amalia."

I say, "Holtz."

I'm afraid he's going to turn me down. Suddenly there's a pre-embarrassed knot in my throat, because this is always how it goes. Maybe I'm just a little too slutty to be interesting. And the experiment is winding down anyway; things are about to come to an end.

It's fine.

I misinterpreted some stuff.

It's fine.

It's. Fine.

But then Ezra just raises his eyebrow, making his expression even more uneven, and he says, "Far be it from me to judge you on your level of halakhic observance."

Now it's my turn to raise an eyebrow.

"But Levitically, we should be dwelling in the sukkah."

My eyebrows climb to my hairline. Because I'm not sure if he's suggesting what I think he's suggesting, but all signs point to him implying that we should.

Well.

Hang out in this open-air temporary structure, which is basically the same thing as *hanging out* outside. In suburbia. In a backyard.

Then again, I don't think I've ever heard someone use the word *Levitically* in a come on. So I could be wrong.

I say, "Levitically?"

"Leviticus 23:42-43. *You shall live in booths seven days—*"

"I know what Sukkot is, Ezra!"

He laughs out loud, and then I'm laughing because I'm a little on edge trying to decide if I'm interpreting him right, and not knowing whether it sounds like the best idea in the world or the worst one. I'm also laughing because I'm so delighted to hear him laugh.

God, what am I doing?

He steps a little closer to me, fingers still pressing into the crook of my elbow. I could slip away if I wanted to but I do *not* want to. I want him to touch me. With his scratched-up hands.

He says, all mischief, "It's a mitzvah, Yaabez."

"Fucking in the sukkah?"

Ezra's eyes are sparkling. "You perv. *Dwelling* in the sukkah."

"Is this like a *known in a Biblical sense* translation thing?"

He shrugs. "I've seen no evidence to the contrary."

"Are you telling me you want to show me your lulav and etrog?"

He's grinning. Full on, genuine. He says, "Is that what the kids are calling it these days?"

I step a little closer to him. Close enough that my thighs are brushing his. A warm breeze blows through the open air side of the sukkah and tickles my legs, ruffles my too-short skirt.

Ezra says, "Well. This gonna work on you?"

"You are the biggest nerd."

"Is that a no?"

"Absolutely not."

He laughs again, throws his head back when he does so I can see his Adam's apple, the tendons at his throat shifting. The shadows of the evening playing over his jaw. Good *lord*. I swallow, or try to.

He looks at me when he's done laughing, adjusts his glasses but for once not in a disapproving way, and I run my hand up his chest, behind his neck, fingers threading through the hair at the base of his neck.

I whisper, because our faces are close enough now that that's all we have to do. He can probably feel it on his mouth when I say, "And here I thought you were such a nice Jewish boy."

He can't stop smiling and I am *living* for it.

"Please. As though my insisting upon halakhic observance changes that." He walks me back until my butt hits the folding table.

"You want to hook up *outside*."

"Only kind of outside."

I shift back until I'm leaning on the plastic, texture digging into my lower back. I don't care.

"Outside enough that now I know you aren't *nice*."

"And I thought you were wild."

"Come find out."

His hands are at my hips and his teeth are at my throat. If you'd asked me, I never, in a million years, would have predicted that this was how Ezra would be.

Overwhelming.

Intoxicating.

All edges, precise and clean and sharp.

He skates his hand up my thigh and slowly, murderously slowly, kneels down in the dirt. His teeth are at my leg, the sensitive inner skin of it that I never bother shaving. Gliding up above my knee until his nose nudges the hem of my skirt.

He murmurs, into my skin, "Yes?"

I say, "God, yes."

And then I'm gone, I'm just *gone*. I don't even have the mental energy to expend on my disbelief that this is Ezra, because I'm so focused on what he's doing, on this kaleidoscope of sensations coursing through me, and screw anyone, *anyone* who thinks I am less because of this.

Who thinks that enjoying this, that craving this, makes me less human.

I don't care about any of it. I don't care about the imminent end of this. I don't care that I'm all wrong for him and we probably both know it and we're just biding our time with each other until a letter grade marks the end of it. I don't care that I am an absolute jumble of feelings I never, *never* intended to feel about Ezra Holtz that I cannot seem to banish from my heart.

I don't. Care.

I care about biting down on my own tongue so I don't make a sound, so we don't disturb his neighbors. I care about getting what we both want from each other right here, right now, in the freaking *sukkah*. I care about everything, every sensation, pinpointing to his hands and his mouth and everything else about him and me and all of this.

Even with my dedicated efforts to be quiet, I can't help this sound rising up in the back of my throat when I rise up on my tiptoes and then finally relax. Ezra looks up at me and scrapes his teeth over his lip, and I'm so freaking high on everything, and what I want, what I really desperately want more than anything, is to reciprocate.

So.

I pull him up to his feet.

And I do.

Here is the terrifying thing.

Here is the thing that has me shaking in my bones.

When we're done, when both of us are so exhausted in the best, most incredible way, when we're high on each other and just cannot feel better than we do, when I know that staying will only be a downhill journey because how can it even *plateau*, I don't want to leave.

Ezra doesn't kick me out.

I stay.

We're lying there on the dirt floor of the little booth, and I'm still feeling just a little self-conscious about the open air to my left, but no cops have shown up so either his neighbors are *very* tolerant, or we were quiet enough and his fence provided enough cover that we're not going to freaking jail.

My head is on Ezra's chest. Ugh, my head is on his chest and I don't want to move it. I'm so comfortable and he's so warm and solid and I love this too much. He's absently running his fingers through my hair, which, I don't even know how; it's a mess, as always. But he manages. And I love it.

I'm so scared, because I love this too much.

I haven't even had the time to begin to contemplate feeling like this, but suddenly I am, and this wasn't supposed to happen.

This doesn't usually happen to me, and it never, never happens to people *about* me, and especially not long-term. Never. So it doesn't matter what random sensations are confusing me right now.

I'm a little scared.

But I'm not scared enough to move.

Ezra is just staring up at the sky through the vine and board roof and so am I. Crickets are singing and the stars are popping out, and that is actually a rule of the sukkah: you have to be able to see the stars through it.

So here I am.

Lying with Ezra, practically purring while he plays with my hair, staring up at the stars.

It's downright romantic.

And there's absolutely nothing to be done for it.

Ezra shifts so I can feel his mouth against my hair. He says, "How you doing?"

I laugh. "How do you think?"

"Well, I'm hoping for the best."

"Good. I feel good."

"What's better? Doing it in the pool house or in the sukkah?"

I laugh again; I can't stop. I'm giddy. Gracious, get it together, me. I say, "Well, hold on. You consider what we did in the pool house sex?"

"Well," he says, "at least sex stuff. What, hands don't count? There's gotta be a penis involved for it to be sex stuff?"

I raise my eyebrows and prop myself up to look him in the eye. "That's progressive for a straight."

He says, "Well, I don't want to brag, but I've read the internet."

"Did you . . . did you do research?"

Even in the dark, I can see his face get a little red. He looks up at the roof and the sky when he says, "I wanted to know what someone like you . . ."

"A queer girl."

"Yeah. What you would call sex."

"And you couldn't just ask me?"

"God, no," he says, and then we're both laughing and it's like a drug. I'm so comfortable, because somewhere along the way I guess I started trusting him.

And there is a huge, massive difference in hooking up with someone you don't know all that well, and hooking up with someone you really, truly trust.

I've done both.

And this . . . this is definitely the latter.

Ezra whispers into my hair, "Tell me something you've never told anyone."

I breathe. I stare at the vines and the little flowers woven around the sparse boards of the roof. The first thing that comes to my mind is so sad that I don't want to say it, but the second I think it, I have to. I say, out loud, "Skylar is my best friend. And I think we're the kind of best friends who don't make it after high school."

Ezra blows out a breath.

I feel an instant hole in my chest. But also a relief. Skylar and I both know it, but we haven't said it and it's sad and I don't know how to fix it or how bad I want to. But I guess I've said it now. To someone.

"I'm sorry," he says. He kisses my hair and it's so tender, so sincere that it makes me want to cry.

"It's okay. Well. It's not okay. But—but in some ways it is. I don't know."

He doesn't ask me anything else about it. And I'm grateful for it because now that it's said, I don't want to take it back exactly, but it's the kind of thing you only have to say out loud once.

I say, "Now you. Tell me something."

"What kind of something?"

"Something you've never told anyone."

He's quiet. Stroking my hair still. Staring up at the sky, watching the stars fade in and out, in and out against the black. He's quiet for so long that I think maybe he won't answer, and I'm enjoying all of this too much to push him.

Then he says, "I'm in love with you."

I stop breathing. "What?"

I feel his heart stutter under my ear.

"I think . . ." His breath shakes. "I'm in love with you, Amalia."

At that second, in which I am completely frozen, the sky opens up and it starts to rain.

It is the perfect reason for me to say, "I have to go."

It feels wrong when I do.

CHAPTER TWENTY-FIVE

Observation: Humans, the Earth, the universe all have one thing in common: the tendency toward self-destruction.

The universe will eventually do it no matter what.

The shitty thing is, if the Earth isn't doing it to itself fast enough, well, people are happy to help it along.

The shittier thing is that we are also, as a species, eager to help each OTHER self-destruct. Billions of people. Billions of sentient DO NOT PRESS. DESTRUCTION IMMINENT buttons, just.

Walking the frick around.

It's a wonder we've made it this far, being so unanimously helpful.

Since Sukkot, Ezra and I have hardly talked. We've seen each other at school and compared data sets and ideas on our project in class. We're getting close to the end of it, very close to drawing all our conclusions and wrapping up our findings on love in a neat presentation. It stings, thinking about that. I want it to be part relief, but it's not.

I haven't texted him since he said it, which makes me feel kind of guilty. It's been a week. And just. Nothing. In fairness, he hasn't texted me either. Or called or just showed up randomly like he apparently does sometimes. I didn't go to temple Friday so who knows if he was there.

What I know is: we are both pretending he didn't say what he said, we are both pretending I didn't get up and immediately leave in response, and we are both terrible at it.

I don't know how to go back to Ezra regarding me coolly, like I am irritating at best. I don't know how to slip back into my casual disdain for this boy who has had his hands everywhere on me, his mouth, who has listened to my secrets and somehow knows me. Like. *Knows* me.

I don't know how it happened and I don't know how to let it go, and what I really don't know is why, exactly, I feel like I need to.

But I do.

It claws at my ribcage, pounds into my veins every time I consider picking up the phone and saying, *Ezra, I don't know what's gotten into me here, but haha obviously I'm in love with you, too.*

Every time it crosses my mind, I start to panic. I think, because I hate the unexpected.

That seems . . . bizarre, when I consider it. I'm like the poster child for impulse; I know that and so does everyone else.

The thing is, when we went cliff-diving, it was *me* who pushed everyone into doing it.

When I decided one afternoon in the eighth grade to walk down to the salon and shave half my head and dye the other half rainbow (to my parents' UTTER disdain), it was a surprise to everyone but me.

When I got high as hell and started a flash mob in the eleventh grade, it was me who organized it.

People don't spring things on me.

People have never, *never* sprung *I'm in love with you* on me, and I keep glancing at Ezra during class, looking for any sign that he's losing his shit like I am, any indication that he meant what he said, that it's real. That he is a total freaking mess.

But he's not. He's caught me looking at him several times and I just blink away and pretend I didn't see him see me and I hate this.

I hate this because I get the feeling that once again, I am ruining everything. That just like I did with Skylar, I'm fucking up all of this.

I am terrified that, despite everything I would have predicted, Ezra Holtz has the potential to be good for me, and I'm so scared of the idea that I'm ruining it. I am *more* terrified that if I give in, if I say, *Holy shit, man, I totally love you, too*, it'll take weeks and the fun, wild me will flake off day by day and Ezra will realize he has been tricked.

He will expect me to leave like I always do, to be this fun, sexy ride that he'll get off of the second he starts to see the rust on the gears.

Well, more than he's seen already.

I guess if anyone has seen anything unsavory about me, it's been him. But I don't . . . No.

I—I can't. I can't give him that opportunity. Ezra Holtz is smart and driven and funny—apparently—and hot and a future engineer. He is perfect, basically. No matter what he thinks about my tits and having access to them, he's not in love with me.

That's not the way this works.

A

I spend the rest of the week being kind of a wet paper towel about everything, Halloween comes, and then it's a weekend studying for a chemistry exam on Monday. Ezra and I professionally and cordially worked out most of our stuff for the project that we're presenting on Thursday, gathered all the data into something cohesive, and he's supposed to finish up the report while I finish our visual aids and take point on the actual presenting. I'm pretty relaxed in front of a crowd, so it made the most sense to divvy it up this way.

I still feel like I'm not entirely equipped for all of this, this life of academia. I still feel kind of like I'm missing something, spending five hours in my room studying what should have taken me thirty minutes because I can't stop getting distracted by the computer. Getting B's on tests I could have maybe gotten A's on if I'd only actually, you know, *spent* that five hours studying instead of shitposting. I still feel the slight burn of shame when I think about majoring in something different than what

I'd planned, but it's not overwhelming anymore. It's a little sting. The way change always feels.

I do still feel just . . . unprepared. For what comes after high school. Like it's all too big—everything, the choices are too huge, too overwhelming. In a few months, all my stories will hearken back to college days, not *Well, when I was in high school*, and people will see me as an adult, which means I should at least have my shit together enough to ace a chemistry test.

But, I don't know.

Maybe everyone feels this way.

Either way, I do.

It's a constant in the back of my brain when I study. During the five minutes at a time I can force myself to focus on formulas and chemical reactions and all these things I am trying so hard to get a recommendation for so I can get into school, I'm also thinking about being terrified.

Something I am good at, as it turns out, is being scared of decisions that mean something.

It's Sunday night, and here I am, studying, when I want to be with friends, when I . . . ugh. When I want to be with Ezra Holtz.

Monday comes and goes, and I do well on the test, I think, and now it is time for my brain to switch gears.

Tuesday morning, I skate into class two minutes late, and Ezra gives me the same look he did the day we were paired and I was late. Dismissive.

I slide into my desk beside him, try not to think about *I'm in love with you, Amalia,* and the goose bumps on my skin at the memory. Try not to let it show on my face that I'm afraid I might be making a huge mistake ignoring it.

I say, "Holtz," without looking at him, because I can't look at him. I know if he really looks at my eyes, he will see me. He will see what's really happening up here in this messed up brain of mine and know, somehow, that what I'm thinking is: *Do you love me? You? HOW. Does it even matter? Not really. If you wait it out long enough, you'll start to feel like you've been fooled. And then. Well. Then, you'll leave.*

So I say it to the dry-erase board up front.

Ezra says, "Amalia."

Even though it's a few minutes past the start of class, kids are still murmuring, readying their projects. Talking to each other. It should be interesting, presentation-wise. I mean, I'm sure some of them will be pairs of Ezras so their projects will be just completely devoid of interest, which basically guarantees them A's but also guarantees that the rest of us will fall asleep. Besides that though, it's psychology. And though it pains me to say this, well, psychology is kind of cool.

Kaylee would be doing straight-up pirouettes if she knew I was transforming into a nerd before her eyes. *Psychology is cool. Chemistry is cool.* Jesus, what's next? *MITOSIS, SPECIFICALLY, IS COOL.* Shit, you know what? It probably is.

"Cutting it close there," says Ezra, and I raise an eyebrow at him.

"Hm?"

"Presentations start in two minutes."

"Okay?"

Ezra's eyes narrow. "Presentations. Start." He leans forward and I glance down at his forearms, his veins, before looking back up at his face. "In two minutes."

"Right, yes, thank you, I can hear."

"Then why aren't you digging in your bag?"

I frown.

Ezra smooths his hand over the pages on his desk—our report.

"It's . . . our presentation is on Thursday," I say.

The color drains from Ezra's face. "What?"

"It's on Thursday."

"Amalia." He turns toward his backpack and yanks the syllabus out. It looks brand new, like it hasn't lived in a backpack for the entire quarter. My stomach hollows and then knots. He reads it off where he scribbled—excuse me, wrote with the precision of a typewriter—next to this assignment: today's date.

Oh my god.

Oh my *god*.

"Ezra," I say, and my mouth hangs open, just a little, so I can breathe.

"You didn't," he says.

"I just . . ." I can feel the panic strangling me, just blocking off my airway and filling my lungs like cement. My head hurts suddenly and it feels huge, it feels irrecoverable. With Ezra staring at me like that, all wide-eyed and lock-jawed. He reaches for his glasses and adjusts them in the most pointed, barely controlled way, and I want to slide under my desk and melt in to the floor. "I thought. I thought it was Thursday. I thought the whole time."

"I said Tuesday! The last time we talked!"

"Which was when, even? We've barely spoken." I say that and hear it the second it leaves my mouth; I'm a moron. That's my fault, too, so like *Here, enemy in war, are you out of ammunition? I'll just toss you some. Yeah, it's cool, my weapon is completely empty.*

Ezra's jaw drops.

I am grateful that he is speechless, because I don't even want to hear what he would otherwise have to say back to *that*.

"I'm sure you said it," I say. "I had this huge chem test and I'm not used to this, and oh my god, Ezra. I'm so sorry. I'm so sorry; can I make this up to you? What do I do?"

Ezra purses his lips. He presses his fingers into the table. He says, in this low, measured voice, "Nothing."

"What do you mean, *nothing*?"

"I'm going to get a pass from the teacher. And I'm going to drive home. My house is three minutes away. When I'm there, I'm going to pick up the draft of the presentation that I have on my computer. I'm going to bring it back here, and you are going to read it off. Take the credit, I don't care. I'm used to it in group projects."

I blink. "You did your own version of my work?"

Ezra doesn't answer. He just looks at me like *Can you blame me?*

And that cuts like a knife. I've been trying so hard. So. Freaking hard. I've been killing myself and trying like hell to turn into this new person and to believe in myself and *work* and Ezra. Ezra Holtz was in love with me, but now I'm sure he's not, and I fucked everything up like I always do, and Ezra. *Ezra* didn't even believe in me.

Once again, I destroyed everything.

And Ezra isn't surprised. Because, like I said, he didn't believe in me.

Who could?

What kind of a total moron *would*?

I feel sick. Like literally physically sick to my stomach, and I raise my hand, not even waiting for the teacher to call on me before I run out of the classroom and down the hall. This is not super surprising, I guess, because I'm on my period today, which means I've already been nauseated since I woke up, but yeah. I get sick in the bathroom.

CHAPTER TWENTY-SIX

Analysis: Available data suggests that, contrary to scientist's initial conjecture, scientist and subject know each other more deeply than they thought.

Available data suggests emotional intimacy.

Available data suggests intense emotion between scientist and subject.

Available data . . . available data is an absolute mess.

Much like the freaking scientist.

Something I hate is that I pride myself in being cool and medium while on my period, because it's shitty when you get like, justifiably mad about something and some dude fires back at you with, "What? Are you on your period?" And I was on my period, and totally overreacted to something.

That just infuriates me.

It doesn't make it less shitty and sexist when dudes do that, but it makes me mad at myself.

Here's the thing, though: period cramps are the worst. Period NAUSEA proves that claim wrong. And all of that combined with intense, sudden anxiety and guilt and some self-worth issues that I probably need therapy for just combined into one giant swirling torrent of "I AM SPRINTING TO THE BATHROOM NOW."

Ezra, at least, had the grace to look a little guilty. A little surprised.

I actually leave class.

I just . . . go home. I call the school after to try to salvage some level of excusal and just pray that the teacher is cool about me skipping out.

Ezra texts me later to say that we're clear, that he talked with the teacher and it's going to be fine, and I text back: *ok*.

That's it.

That's Tuesday.

Skylar comes over on Wednesday while I work and tells me about her girlfriend and how maybe they're going to break up, because they're going to be going to different colleges anyway, and should they? Or is that stupid?

I'm listening and working at the same time.

I feel like kind of a crappy friend because I should be paying more attention. I should want to tell her about Ezra and all the total stress I am putting on myself about it and the disaster that was Tuesday. I should tell her all these things, but I don't want to.

And that, *that* is why I said what I said to Ezra in the sukkah: that I love Skylar now, but that maybe we are the friends who drift after we don't see each other at school every day.

I don't know.

Maybe that's shitty.

Maybe it's okay.

I'm here with her now, though. She's on the carpet being a good friend who's not thinking about the inevitable dissolution of our friendship one day and I have no idea why I even am, and . . . I close my laptop.

I'll stay up late tonight to finish.

I say, "I'm sorry, Sky. Say that last thing again?"

Because goddammit. Whatever happens with us, whatever kind of friends we are ultimately meant to be, I love her.

And she matters.

♗

On Thursday, Ezra is waiting outside before class starts. We're the first ones to present and we only have five minutes so I'm not expecting him to do anything but disapprove of whatever time I show up.

Back to old times.

That's not what happens.

Ezra brushes his fingers over my elbow and I stop, just in front of the door. That turns out to be a stupid choice, because kids keep shoving past us to get in and we waste a good sixty seconds just being jostled. Eventually, we relocate to the lockers.

"What?" I say. It comes out more forcefully, more annoyed, than I mean it to. Ultimately, he hasn't done much wrong. He thinks he's in love with me and there's no way he is, but how am I going to fault him for that, I guess? He didn't have any faith in me. Made the totally jackass move of having a full backup because he *expected* me to screw everything up, and that . . . well. It doesn't feel great.

But I can't be too pissed about that either. Because I *did* screw things up. I'm frustrated with him—what else is new?—but I guess more than anything, I'm furious at myself.

For eight billion different reasons. And that is why my *What* comes out more like a *WHAT*.

Ezra doesn't flinch. I don't know why that's attractive.

He just stares down at me and says, "I'd like to talk with you."

"Now?" I blink up at the clock in the hall. "We have two minutes until the bell rings."

"After the presentation. After school. I'd like to come over and talk with you. Is that something you would agree to?"

He's so formal, but it doesn't sound stilted; it's sounds smooth. Practiced. It sounds like one of the hundred versions of Ezra Holtz I have come to intimately know over the years.

I say, while my mind processes that thought: "Not today. I have a family thing. Tomorrow?"

He scrapes his teeth over his lip.

"My parents are going out, but we can light candles at my place if that's something you're concerned about." I'm sure he is. Tomorrow night is Shabbat.

"Yeah," he says. "Okay. Tomorrow."

He runs his hand through his hair, and that gesture is so breathtakingly familiar to me now that it actually aches. Like I've lost something when he disappears into the classroom just as the bell rings.

Even though I didn't lose it; I never *really* had it to begin with.

I'm thinking all of this over while I walk into the classroom.

While I sit at my desk and unpack everything we need for the presentation, while I watch Ezra walk in that long, confident stride to the front of the classroom and hand in our paper. We've worked our asses off on it, given up countless nights compiling data, wrestling with our differences (and well . . . each other, depending on the mood) and now here we are. Everything is over and life can rewind back to normal.

But I can't keep my eyes off him, can't stop rehashing him looking up at the stars and saying, casually, like it's nothing, *I'm in love with you, Amalia.* I can't stop thinking about the way he's made me feel and wondering how on Earth it was Ezra Holtz who was responsible for all of this. Wondering what he meant, what he was actually feeling when he made that confession and how it's all going to topple down.

Wondering how, if we did decide to make a run of this, we would get through it without murdering each other.

Not that it matters, not that it's relevant, because it's not going to happen.

I just . . . it can't.

Not with someone like him, and someone like me.

The teacher introduces us and tells me as I walk with Ezra up to the front that he's glad I'm feeling better.

I nod and force a smile and clear my throat. Face my classmates.

I talk slow because I chatter when I'm nervous and I need to do well. For Ezra.

For me.

I want to slow all of this down anyway. Want to experience us as partners before he comes over tomorrow and we really, finally end things.

I say, "We did our project on an updated version of Arthur Aron's *The Experimental Generation of Interpersonal Closeness*. A study that posited that anyone could fall in love with anyone, if they got to know each other well enough."

Ezra clicks to the next slide and cuts in, "We made our own set of questions intended to generate intimacy in the same way Arthur Aron did, and matched up volunteers based on what we determined to be factors of compatibility."

We go through the traits we chose that might deem a couple compatible. Our methodology as far as determining those factors, the questions.

My stomach hurts, not because I'm nervous about public speaking. That's the number one fear of Americans, above death, even, but it's never really been one of mine.

My stomach hurts because as Ezra goes down the list on the screen, question by question, I realize I know every single one of his answers. I know the smell that makes him the happiest (petrichor—when rain falls after a dry spell), I know his very worst memory (his best friend, Moshe, was in a car accident in the eighth grade and died. I remember standing beside him in services while he chose to say kaddish, even though he didn't have to. I remember the time right after it happened when Ezra showed up at youth group, and I was the only one dragging behind when we all left the room to go do who knows what, and wound up basically alone with Ezra and he just broke down. That was maybe the first time I ever touched him on purpose. I had forgotten that specific touch, but I remember it now). I know if he could change one thing about the way he was raised, what it would be (he would have siblings). I know that his favorite thing about himself is his passion, even though I never would have read that on him before, but now it's so obvious. It's so obvious that it *always* should have been obvious. He cares about things. About people. Deeply.

We are up here presenting on our findings and my brain is now working out where exactly, and to whom, that passion might extend. It's working out whether Ezra Holtz could possibly be in love with me.

Worse than that . . . it's not working out *if* I've fallen in love with him.

It's working out *when*.

I blink when it becomes clear that Ezra has been waiting for me to speak for a moment. He's ready to jump in, I think, to take over when it's clear I'm lost in thought.

But he doesn't.

He waits for me.

I clear my throat. "As for the ultimate findings," I say, "our first couple is still a couple. They claim to love each other. They seem compatible and happy and the intimacy established through the experiment seems to prove Aron's—and our—hypothesis. Our second couple is no longer together romantically. While there is some attraction still reported, it was determined by the subjects that friendship was where their relationship made the most sense. Both respondents, however, claimed, when asked, that it was absolutely fair to say they loved each other. Not romantically, but in a very real platonic sense. As for our third couple, they did nothing to prove our hypothesis, as they hated each other from the beginning, and they hate each other now."

"Sometimes," Ezra says, "getting to intimately know a person really doesn't help if you hate everything you find out. Even with the failsafe of mirror neurons and empathy that the staring for four minutes into one another's eyes was supposed to generate."

There's a low wave of laughter from the class.

"I'll point out for the record," I say, "that it was me who insisted on matching that couple. Ezra maintained that it was doomed to fail."

Ezra smiles smoothly for the class and says, "She's right."

"Mark that down on the calendar," I call back before I think about it, "I'm right."

Ezra glances at me and he looks surprised. Caught entirely off-guard. He fixes his face in an instant and turns back to the class, and I am left with my pulse crashing under my skin.

Ezra says, "While the results of the study weren't uniform, it did begin to prove that emotional intimacy, while it may not always generate love—"

"Even compulsory intimacy," I cut in.

"Yes," says Ezra. "Even when it was circumstantial, it does generate strong emotional connection, positive or negative."

"Which really," I say, "is the basis of love."

Ezra meets my eyes when I say it, and I stutter. As the class claps politely and I stand there frozen, and so does he, all I want is to leave. Right here, right now.

But then . . . maybe all I want to do is stay.

CHAPTER TWENTY-SEVEN

Observation: In nature, family bonds are observed as oft-beneficial tools for physical safety and thus the perpetuation of the species. All precise functions of the family unit, particularly when said family unit may be risky (as in the case of lions eating their young, or in the case of my trying to quietly exist while Ben ruins all our hearing with outdated Irish punk) are unclear.

In cases unlike the lion, in cases of family units that weave together in emotional and physical support, the lengths of such bonds are unquantifiable.

But relationships function like they do for a reason.

I cannot quantify everything I get from mine. But god, am I glad they exist.

Irish punk and all.

I pull in the driveway after school and I don't know if I'm glad to have had the excuse not to see Ezra tonight or frustrated.

I have a solid couple hours of homework (AP classes are the devil) ahead of me, so it's probably a good thing. If I knew he was going to be here tonight, I wouldn't be able to focus.

I can barely focus now.

Who am I kidding—I can barely focus enough to get all this Smart People shit done when I'm totally neutral.

Ben would slap me upside the head for calling it *Smart People shit* and say, "Smart People shit was made for you, dude."

Maybe not Smart People shit.

Motivated People shit.

People who know how the frick to manage their heads and time because they haven't skated by on the least possible effort for eleven years shit.

I sigh, and I kill the engine.

I head inside.

I don't even say hi to my family, because I can't afford to get caught in any conversation that might hold my interest for more than fifteen minutes. If I start talking, I'll use it as an excuse to *stay* talking and then I won't finish my chem homework, or I'll employ my second most typical strategy which is: do everything at four a.m., turn it in in a state of total disarray, and walk away with a C. B, maybe.

It takes all my self-control to shut myself in my room, and more than that to actually open my AP chem book, but I do it because I know once I start, I'll actually be interested. It's so bizarre to actually care about this kind of stuff now that I've forced my eyes to open to it, but I do.

I open the book.

I flip to the section on bonding, and my brain clicks on after five minutes. This—this is how I know this is the right call for me, major-wise. My mind doesn't do this in literature, it doesn't do this in bio, in algebra. I skate through those things like everything else, and by *skate through* I mean *barely*. I mean, even now that I'm *trying*, I sleep through all of them.

This, though, I guess I really do enjoy it.

Who knew a person could like more than one thing?

I work on chem, on bio, on lit, everything but psych because I finally have a break. And when it's through, I head upstairs where the whole floor smells like maple chile chicken. Spices and sweet. Kaylee is roasting some green beans in the oven, and I just stand there for a while and inhale.

I miss being a part of this.

I barely have the time to be right now; it's like I haven't even left for college and I'm already practically gone. But it's okay. At least Thanksgiving break is coming kind of soon and then I can participate with everyone again.

This is temporary.

It's for something I need.

It's okay.

"Hey, stranger," says Dad.

I set the table for something to do with my hands, to make myself feel like I'm participating in family dinner beyond eventually consuming it, and sit at the table.

Mom dishes out the food and everyone eats, and I relax.

Man. I had no idea until just now how freaking keyed up I've been.

"You feelin' okay, Molls?" says Ben.

I shrug and say, "I'll live."

Kaylee says, "Too much studying will rot your brain, you know."

I roll my eyes but I'm smiling. "You're one to talk."

"Please." She tosses her long, shiny hair out of her eyes. "As if I need to study."

"Okay, nerd," says Ben, and Mom laughs, and it's nice. That even when my life is in flux, when Ezra is a complete massive question mark and I love my best friend but can't always tell if we're good for each other, when school is a jumble of questions and uncertainty, when I'm so stretched thin by eight thousand responsibilities that I can barely participate in our life, I still have this.

This. My people are always the same.

I relax.

I breathe.

I eat.

⚗

After dinner, we pile on the couches and watch *The Last Jedi* for the ninetieth time, and after the third time that Dad insists he wasn't sleeping, he was just resting his eyes, and Kaylee is passed out so deeply that she doesn't even wake up when she flops off the couch and onto the floor, I head back into my room.

Books are all over the floor, college apps stuffing my computer with window after window, most of which read:

Submitted. I've sent in apps to a few state schools, a few community colleges—backups and slight reaches. I can't go far enough to finish out any kind of advanced chem degree at a community college, but I could at least snag a number of gen eds, prove I can work, then move forward if I need to.

I have options.

I can make a career out of science. I can take a few classes in art, minor in it. I don't know, that art restoration route is looking better and better all the time. Maybe . . . maybe later I double-major; who knows.

But right now, this is the plan.

And it's . . . honestly? It's okay.

I play with the hem of my oversized night shirt and consider going to bed. Even step toward it. Then I feel a tug in my chest. One I haven't felt in a long time. Not over the pain of it.

But it's there, pulling. Hard. Hard enough I can't go to sleep.

I turn toward my easel and pull out a blank canvas.

It's after eleven, it's a school night. But I don't care.

I get out my supplies and sit in front of the easel.

For the first time in months, I paint.

CHAPTER TWENTY-EIGHT

Pre-Experiment Hypothesis: Love is predictable. If a specific set of factors of compatibility, and stimuli that generate levels of intimacy, are employed, then love can be created. Predicted. We know there is a formula; it is not complicated, when it comes down to it.

Post-Experiment Conclusion: We don't know shit.

Friday night, my parents are out. Ben is hanging out inside somewhere, probably playing video games or something, and Kaylee is with him, probably making fun of his video game addiction while simultaneously getting totally sucked into the story. If she hasn't already, by the end of the night, she will have snaked the controller from him and commandeered the whole thing.

I am thinking about this, about familiar patterns and things that calm me, because Ezra will be here any minute.

We haven't texted since Thursday, except for me saying: *whenever you get here, just meet me at the treehouse*

And Ezra responding: *Okay.*

That period freaks me out. Who knew a piece of punctuation so tiny could bring forth so many tonal possibilities?

I'm so anxious, way more than is characteristic for me. I just . . . I wish I knew what was going to happen tonight. Wish I had any clue at all which way this was going to shake out. Wish I had . . . control.

I hear the dull hum of an engine, the putter as it dies. My heart jumps up into my esophagus.

I dig my nails into my palms then loosen, dig then loosen. My stomach is swooping and hollowing and tightening.

I hear Ezra's feet crunching over the leaves.

Oh god.

Here we go.

He raps his knuckles on the tree and I say, "Come up."

He climbs.

Pops his head into the treehouse then hoists himself up and in, and for seconds, neither of us says anything.

We just . . . stare.

I don't know what to say or how to say it. It's not like we're fighting, really. Not like we broke up because we were never together to begin with.

Not like either of us is furious or something; we're just . . . frozen.

Hovering in limbo.

Who is supposed to talk?

I look at his jaw, the sharp cut of his cheekbones, those black-framed glasses I have grown so used to, his slightly too-long hair. My pulse is racing.

Ezra cracks first.

"Amalia, I just . . . I need you to know that I didn't have a whole project backed up."

That is not what I expected him to say.

"What?" I say.

"Just—I didn't. I started my own stuff way back when we began this whole thing, before we'd started to really work together. When you showed up hung over to study with me, and that guy was inviting you to more parties and you seemed down for all of it. I didn't—yeah. I didn't trust you, and why should I have?"

I wrinkle my nose but don't interrupt.

"I realized the more we worked that you actually did care and I had you all wrong, and I stopped. I swear. What I had was bare bones, nothing close to what you churned out. It was shitty of me, maybe, to make a backup in the first place, but I swear it wasn't because I didn't have any faith in you or something. It was because I didn't at first. And I was wrong."

"Well," I say. My throat is dry. I make a valiant attempt at swallowing. "Not that wrong. I messed up."

He runs a hand through his hair, brushes his fingers over his glasses on the way, like he does when he's nervous. "It's forgivable."

"Yeah?"

"You did something we all do. I was pissed at the time, but you pulled through, and our grade is going to be fine. I just—I couldn't stand you thinking I'd basically been lying to you this whole time."

"Okay," I say. I blink outside, where the sun is just beginning to set. "Is that it?"

Ezra blows out a breath. He looks out at the sky, too. In a second, it will be streaked with pink and orange. Right now, it's just . . . waiting.

He says, to the sky, "Sure."

And then I realize: I do not want him to go.

It's not him who has things to say.

It's me.

I say, too fast, "You'll never make it home before sunset. Light candles with me."

Ezra furrows his brow and stares at me. Then says, "Okay."

I strike the match I brought, light the Shabbat candles and set them in the treehouse window. I cover my eyes and say the blessing—I try to sing it, jury's out as to whether I'm successful.

The sun sets.

The sky streaks with celestial paint.

We are both quiet again, left with sundown and candlelight and . . . a number of memories we have from this treehouse.

The air is thick with them.

I say, finally, because if we are quiet for too long, he'll leave and I—I can't have him leave. I don't want him to go.

I say, "Holtz?"

"Yeah?"

"When you told me you loved me."

He hisses out air through his teeth. "Jesus." He's embarrassed. I mean, yeah. Sure.

"I said I had to go."

"I recall."

I'm shaking? Yeah. I'm shaking. "I don't know how the hell this happened but I guess—" I can barely say it because how *did* it happen? And what if I ruined everything with my freak out? "Ezra. I don't . . ." I rub my hand over my forehead.

I wanted to control this whole thing so bad and now I can't. Now the words are sticking in my throat.

Ezra cuts in: "Amalia, do you know that I've been in love with you forever?"

I choke. "What?"

"Forever."

"I thought—" I can barely breathe. He's staring straight at me, not even nervous anymore, just sure. Intent. Focused, like he always is. Maybe there really is something to those mirroring neurons, because something is happening to me at the chemical level. "I thought you thought I was irritating."

He laughs. A real smile. My insides light up.

"Yeah. Of course I did. You irritate the shit out of me."

Now it's my turn to laugh and I don't know if it's a release of tension or the coiling of it.

"We've known each other since we were kids and I just . . . I was always fascinated by you. Even when you were making me nuts. You had all these maddening ideas and were this . . . just totally wild, weird person and you were *interesting*. But then after . . . after Moshe."

I nod.

His voice cracks on it.

"That night. At youth group. You were there and no one else was. I knew you half-hated me and you just sat

there with me and touched me and you cared. I think . . .
I don't know. I don't know if I fell for you then or if it was
before or after or what. But I know that I've been in love
with you for years."

My throat constricts. I legit cannot breathe. My palms
are sweating and I just—how. *How.* I say, "I haven't been in
love with you forever. You really did make me crazy, Ezra."

"Well, don't sugarcoat things to spare my feelings."

"But I can't stop thinking about you."

"About wringing my neck?"

"About kissing it."

His eyes go dark.

"I feel like . . . like I don't know anyone as well as I
know you. It freaks me out, like maybe I'll fall head over
heels for you and then you'll realize I'm not who you th—"

"Your favorite food is chocolate-covered raisins. You
freak."

I close my mouth.

He says, "You love the darkest nature docs, and you
love the bassoon. LOVE. The freaking bassoon. Who loves
the bassoon?"

I laugh. I can't stop laughing.

He's naming all the oddest things about me and that
makes me nervous until he says: "Your favorite color is
blue. You love pumpkin spice lattes. Nothing makes you
madder than cowardice. You're a Scorpio. I lied. I don't
know that because of the Chanukah thing; I know because
I love you. That's it. I know you."

I breathe out. Low and slow. "You . . . yeah. Yeah, you
really do."

He just waits.

Looks at me.

I say, into the quiet: "God, what the shit. I love you, too."

Ezra laughs.

He laughs harder.

He reaches for my neck and pulls me toward him and laughs into my mouth, and I thread my fingers through his hair.

The candles burn behind us as the sunset gives way to nighttime.

He doesn't leave until long after the candles have burned out.

ACKNOWLEDGMENTS

Kissing Ezra Holtz is, to date, the most difficult story I have ever written. While I was drafting it, I was diagnosed with major depressive disorder (and let me just tell you, as it turns out, brains and their functionality are KIND OF important to, you know. Functioning. Look, we've all learned something today). It was absolutely the most intense episode of depression I've ever dealt with, and what that means is that finishing a story like this, a story that is a huge part of my heart, when it was a real struggle every single day, is something I am so intensely proud of. And that is part of what makes this story, specifically, such a huge team effort.

To all of you who helped yank me into life when it seemed . . . more than difficult, in a hundred different ways, THANK YOU. To Sara Taylor Woods, ˜*˜wife˜*˜, for about a million things, not the least of which was the sukkah scene, you utter perv. To Colleen Oakes, I miss the *heck* out of you; thank you for giving me the idea to tell the story of an artist who is told no in the first place. To Tabitha Martin, for phone call after phone call and talking writing with me and over a decade of friendship. And to Rae Loverde, for hours and hours of talking about books and life and everything else under the sun, and talking about characters like they're real people because DANGIT to US they are. To my therapist, Meghan Gordon—without you stepping in and helping me change the entire course of my life, I never would have been able to tell this story.

My agent, Steven Salpeter, for believing in me and in my work sometimes more than I do. You have no idea how grateful I am for our partnership. Holly Frederick and Maddie Tavis, thank you so much for everything above and beyond that you do. My editor, Nicole Frail, you always have incredible insight and every story we get to work on together only makes me happier that we get to partner in this. To the entire team at Sky Pony—artists, editors at every stage, publicity, production, everything. Thank you for making this dream of mine continually possible.

Bookish community, YA Twitter, Jewish!Twitter, book bloggers, and readers who make this all real, ALL ALL ALL of my love.

And last, to my boys. My kids, you make everything worth it. Harry, thank you, as always, for being the reason I tell love stories.